So That You May Live

BOOK THREE

By
Denise M. Walker

SCRIPTURE

"I shall not die, but I shall live, and recount the deeds of the LORD"
(Psalm 118:17).

DEDICATION

This book is dedicated to all the women who may have encountered obstacles in life. I pray that you will choose to L.I.V.E. out your purpose in the power of Christ.

To my sister-friend, Mary Harris, this one's for you.

A LETTER FROM THE AUTHOR

To the reader,

Thank you for choosing to read So That you May Live. This novel is book three of The Redemption series, Hannah's story. Her story began in 2018 when I pinned the YA novella, Hannah's Hope.

Then, it continued when I released Hannah's Heart in 2019. I have now completed her story in three women's Christian installments (Barren Womb, Sufficient Grace, and So That you May Live).

God gave me the vision of Hannah through a dream several years ago. In the dream, someone was interviewing me about a story I had written with a character named Hannah. At the time, I had not written any fiction. I prayed about it, and asked for direction on what God wanted me to do.

First, I was instructed to go to I Samuel 1:2 and look up the meaning of Hannah's name, which means "grace." God helped me to understand that grace is for all who will receive it. Next, I was given further instructions to use elements of what I had personally experienced to craft her story and help women see His love and grace for them, and I obeyed.

As I have written, the LORD has given me topics that many may not want to address, but there are women and girls around the world dealing with these issues, and He wants to heal and deliver them.

Throughout the women's fiction series, I have covered topics from abuse, endometriosis, broken relationships, forgiveness, and more.

In So That you May Live, I have covered the topic of domestic violence. This is not the only topic Addressed in the story, but it does lead to tragedy. Therefore, I wanted to make you aware before you begin.

I pray that those who read this story will be moved to compassion and will know that God made you in His own image. He loves you, and He has called you to purpose and greatness. Do not accept anything less than His best.

COPYRIGHT

Copyright © 2024 Denise M. Walker So That You May Live
ISBN: 979-8-9910173-0-5

All rights reserved. No part of this book may be reproduced, distributed, or transmitted in any form or by any means, including photocopying, recording, nor by an electronic or mechanical means, including information storage and retrieval systems, without the written permission of the publisher, or the owner of the copyright, except for the use of quotations in a book review. This is a work of fiction. Names. Characters, and incidents are the product of the author's imagination or are used fictitiously. Any resemblance to actual persons, living or dead, events, or locales is entirely coincidental.

The ESV® Bible (The Holy Bible, English Standard Version®) copyright © 2001 by Crossway Bibles, a publishing ministry of Good News Publishers. ESV Text Edition: 2016. The ESV® text has been reproduced in cooperation with and by permission of Good News Publishers. Unauthorized reproduction of this publication is prohibited. All rights reserved.

Publisher: Armor of Hope Writing & Publishing Services

Cover Design: Denise M. Walker

Editor: Chandra Sparks Splond

Table of Contents

PROLOGUE 1
CHAPTER ONE 7
CHAPTER TWO 12
CHAPTER THREE 17
CHAPTER FOUR 21
CHAPTER FIVE 29
CHAPTER SIX 39
CHAPTER SEVEN 49
CHAPTER EIGHT 57
CHAPTER NINE 61
CHAPTER TEN 72
CHAPTER ELEVEN 77
CHAPTER TWELVE 86
CHAPTER THIRTEEN 93
CHAPTER FOURTEEN 101
CHAPTER FIFTEEN 112
CHAPTER SIXTEEN 117
CHAPTER SEVENTEEN 123
CHAPTER EIGHTEEN 130
CHAPTER NINETEEN 137
CHAPTER TWENTY 144
CHAPTER TWENTY-ONE 156
CHAPTER TWENTY-TWO 164
CHAPTER TWENTY-THREE 168
CHAPTER TWENTY-FOUR 175
CHAPTER TWENTY-FIVE 183
CHAPTER TWENTY-SIX 188
CHAPTER TWENTY-SEVEN 195

CHAPTER TWENTY-EIGHT 205
CHAPTER TWENTY-NINE 214
EPILOGUE 220
ABOUT THE AUTHOR 223
OTHER BOOKS BY THIS AUTHOR 224

PROLOGUE

A fog. That's what this feels like. A thick, dense fog. How scary is this? As I attempt to walk the path to the vision you have given me, I feel I am lost in a fog. I can't see the obstacles ahead, not even those just steps away from me, Lord. I'm struggling because I want to be able to see through it and know what's coming, but I must trust that my faith in you will bring me through in the right direction. This is so uncomfortable. Lord, give me the strength to do this, Hannah Jefferson prayed as she closed her eyes and took a calming breath, wanting to get up and leave Pastor Neal Dickerson's conference room and never look back, but how could she run from God's calling? There was nowhere to hide. Yes, she was surely having a Jonah moment. Jonah was the dude in the Bible who tried to do the same thing she was considering. He attempted to run from God's calling.

Pastor Dickerson was one of her board members for the women's development center she'd been tasked by God to open, and he had become a mentor along this journey. The center was to be named the So That You May Live Women's Development Center. It was inspired by the organization she'd founded a few years ago, That You May Live. Hannah had added *So* at the beginning because it sounded better to her, and it was more meaningful. The women she desired to help were women who hadn't had a perfect life but who were women who needed the tools to overcome their current and past hurdles, so they would live and not die without their purpose fulfilled. She had to admit this was one of the hardest steps she'd ever taken.

Hannah and the board had been meeting at Pastor Dickerson's church for the past three months, and she hadn't made much more progress with establishing sustainable funding in order to open. She was elated to have had the ability to invest so much in becoming an entrepreneur and learning about opening a nonprofit organization, but she wanted to give up. When she first got the vision to open a center more than six months ago, she was determined to obey what God had placed in her spirit, but now she questioned if she was ready to take such a big step, so every day since she'd felt more pressed to move forward, she'd been asking God, *Why me? Isn't there someone else who could do something so daring?*

Her nerves were uneasy, but she did her best to focus today. There were only four members of the board. That was all she needed for the moment. In today's meeting, she didn't like the expressions on the faces of Aubrey Young and Dr. Elizabeth Battle, two of the other board members. Hannah knew she shouldn't judge someone by what their mood appeared to be, but their scowls didn't help. She hoped they would stick around and assist her with seeing this vision through.

The board chair was Pastor Dickerson. He pastored Greater Love Ministries, an affiliate with her church, Giver of Life Ministries. The co-chair was Pastor Carolyn Gibson, the director of House of Hope Women's Shelter where Hannah had volunteered for years now. Aubrey had agreed to be the accountant for the center after hearing the vision and falling in love with it. She was affiliated with Pastor Dickerson's church, and she came highly recommended by several of his members, having been their accountant for years. Dr. Battle, the secretary, was a family therapist friend of her mother-in-law's, Mama Jefferson.

She even had two volunteers lined up. Her friend, Tamela Love, was a member of Hannah's church. They had attended a few women's ministry events together over the past year and had become inseparable. Tamela had come into Hannah's life at the right time after her longtime friend had moved away. Her best friend, Robin, had left Georgia when her husband was offered a better paying job in Charlotte, North Carolina. Oh, how she missed her friend. Robin was one of her greatest supporters. She would often help Hannah prepare for her women's mentoring workshops and would also attend them over at House of Hope Women's Shelter. Tamela was much like Robin. She had become a close friend to Hannah, a joy to be around, supportive, and a woman of God. Hannah enjoyed hanging out with her. She had already helped Hannah with preparation for marketing her business website, and she had assisted in many areas at their church. April Evans was a member of Pastor Dickerson's church. Her heart for women was what had connected Hannah to her, and April's and Hannah's daughter, Ariel, attended the same ballet studio and had met a few times for playdates.

Yes, she had all the help she needed, but she still didn't feel prepared.

"After directing the shelter for several years now, I think it's going to take more funding than we are budgeting for to assure the center's success, if we could get more donors to stand behind you, regardless of you being a new nonprofit," Pastor Gibson said.

"Agreed," Pastor Dickerson said.

"What happens if you only get in more small grants?" Aubrey asked.

"I would just have to wait to open," Hannah said.

"No, we are going to do everything to help you obey God," Pastor Gibson said. "You have been a blessing for the women of House of Hope, and this community of women needs an organization to empower them like the one God has given you."

"Well, one of the things you may have to do is eliminate the idea of a receptionist and think of more ways to get in some volunteers. That could definitely help. It's free," Pastor Dickerson said.

"Agreed," Pastor Gibson and Aubrey said.

Hannah agreed as well, but she also knew that meant she would be taking up that slack. It wasn't like anyone here had the time to put in and assist, but she was the director, so it would be her.

"I can talk to a few more members at my church who may want to volunteer," Pastor Dickerson added. "We have to take away something. If the funding you have applied for comes in, that gives you the opportunity to purchase career training and development software for the computers that were donated."

"Yes, that is very important to the vision of the center. I would also love to someday be blessed with newer computers because the donated ones move really slow," Hannah said.

The board members nodded in agreement, the weight of the situation evident on their faces. Hannah appreciated that they all seemed passionate about the center's mission and were equally invested in finding a solution.

"Ideally, it would be great if you could hire more staff—and you will one day," Dr. Battle said, "but the way funding is coming in, it is just not an option."

Hannah sighed, acknowledging the financial reality she faced. Plus, the social media campaigns Tamela had helped her launch were only bringing in small donations at the moment.

"I have another idea for ongoing fundraising. I could host a bake-off periodically, and there is no real cost involved. It could bring in small amounts of money—every bit can help. My mom and mother-in-law have both agreed to participate and donate all their sales to the center. One of my aunts has also agreed to help out," Hannah said, determination creeping into her voice. "I don't know if you know anyone else who would be willing to help."

"You know we love to eat around here, especially some well-made desserts. I'm sure my wife would love to help, and I have a few church mothers over at Greater Love who can throw down in the kitchen," Pastor Dickerson said, rubbing his extended belly and laughing.

Hannah shook her head, grinning. She hadn't heard anyone use the phrase *throw down* in a long time.

"That would be great. Do you think they would be willing to give a portion of their sales to the center?" Hannah asked.

"I could ask."

"I know a few women who can make some good ole southern baked goods," Dr. Battle said.

Hannah nearly cheered. "Could you find out if they would participate and email or text me?"

"Sure."

"I had another thought," Hannah continued. "What if I considered offering internships? That would help me maintain consistent volunteers and save money as well."

That sounds great," Aubrey said. "We could help you reach out to local colleges and universities for students interested in gaining experience in the field of social work and community service management."

"That's what I was thinking. You could provide valuable training and mentorship to young professionals while the center benefits at the same time," Pastor Dickerson added.

"And it won't cost a dime," Aubrey said.

The board members nodded in agreement, seeming a little more energized by the great ideas discussed. Hannah had to admit that offering internships could not only address her funding challenges but also assist with more community involvement and support for the center.

"I'll start reaching out to the colleges and universities right away," Hannah said, feeling a renewed sense of hope.

As the board discussed the logistics of implementing the internship program, another idea surfaced.

"What if we reach out to our network of community partners?" Pastor Gibson suggested. "Perhaps some of them have the skills and expertise to take on temporary roles until we secure more stable funding."

Hannah smiled at the suggestion. "Yes, that could work."

Before concluding the board meeting, Hannah and the board brainstormed potential volunteers who could fill the vacant roles temporarily. The mood in the room had shifted, and Hannah was glad about it, but she was still uneasy with so many unknowns. She thanked the board once again for their great support with the So That You May Live vision, but Hannah still felt she wasn't ready. There seemed to be too many risks involved, and she didn't like it. As a teacher, she didn't have to wonder about any of what they had discussed. She had a steady income and didn't have to worry about possible funding and all that was involved with this.

She was at least armed with the plan to offer internships and the favor of being able to tap into Pastor Dickerson's and Pastor Gibson's network if needed, but she just didn't know. *Lord, please provide more funding as soon as possible,* she prayed as she headed to her car. *Maybe this is not a reality for me right now.* For the moment, Hannah might have to wait and deal with the craziness of what the field of education was becoming.

CHAPTER ONE

A Year Later

This chaos is far from normal, Hannah screamed inside. The field she once loved continued to shift in the wrong direction.

Her ninth year in the classroom, and teachers were absent every other day, and for some reason the district was having trouble getting substitutes to cover classes. Teachers not showing up had everything to do with exhaustion. Parents weren't as supportive as they had been when she began teaching. Even the kids' behaviors and motivations had changed. Hannah had prided herself on being pretty good with classroom management and growing her students in reading and writing, but even the literacy scores had declined year after year. Many talked about it being the pandemic, but Hannah didn't fully agree.

This decline began before the pandemic. Not to mention, the pandemic was a few years ago, so why do things seem to be getting worse? Shouldn't they be getting better? Hannah frowned, glaring at the wall-to-wall students in her room today. *I am so over this.*

The only thing she was grateful for was that the most challenging student she'd ever taught was absent. Hannah breathed a sigh of relief, thanking God she didn't have to deal with Jamal today. He was an angry young man and would often slam things on the floor, push, and intimidate the other students.

Hannah had sent him to the office a number of times. Their principal or assistant principal would talk to him and send him right back to class. It had gotten more and more frustrating by the day.

The time is now. You've delayed long enough, Hannah suddenly heard in her spirit as she took a seat at her desk, caressing her temple. *Not again, Lord.* God had been pressing her to come out of the classroom for over a year now and open her women's center under the organization she'd formed to mentor women and host empowerment workshops, but she still hadn't secured the amount of funding she needed to be comfortable enough to leave her teaching career, no matter how crazy it was at the moment.

In truth, Hannah had given up trying to secure more funding a few months ago. She had grown frustrated with the entire process. When the Lord first placed it on her heart, she was ready to take off running in it, but as time passed, the responsibilities on her plate seemed to be too much, and applying for funding was the worst part because she was a new organization. How could she get any experience if she wasn't given a chance and not scrutinized so much?

With a now three-year-old, a husband, and bills, she felt she needed to wait a little longer, at least until Ariel went to pre-K. So, that had been her constant response to God and to the board. Yes, they had done a lot of legwork, but she still wasn't ready. Hannah didn't understand why God couldn't seem to see her full plate at the moment. Yes, things were getting a little rough being in the classroom, but she couldn't just up and leave.

How would that even work? What about my steady income? What if I never get enough funding to last me a year or two?

Hannah had been waiting ten minutes for an administrator to show up to her room after the fight she'd broken up between two young ladies who were guests in her classroom. Today she had thirty-two students, which had become the norm. There were four teachers out, and Hannah was beyond tired.

This can't keep happening. Some changes have to be made. The problem was it was happening everywhere in education at the moment. She couldn't count how many teachers she'd seen on social media with the same complaints.

Things had seemed to get progressively worse since completing all of her training for opening the women's center. *Is it just a coincidence?* Hannah was all around annoyed. She didn't want to think about doing anything else right now.

The time is now. The words came again.

Lord, I need a steady income, she thought, attempting to negotiate with God for what seemed like the hundredth time. *I can't put everything on Levi's shoulders.*

Hannah had attempted to teach the reading lesson twice now with very little success.

I need this day to be over soon.

Trying to keep her cool, Hannah stood and walked to the front of the room. She'd made all the students put their heads down, and no one could talk, or they would serve an after-school detention with her. She'd sent one of the girls to the class of Mr. Rutherford, another one of the fifth-grade teachers, to cool off. The other remained with her. Hannah could see the attitude written all over her face. Now standing before the class, Hannah attempted to salvage this morning again.

"Alright, ladies and gentlemen, since we have so many students today and everyone has had a chance to settle down, let's attempt to play a reading review game."

"Don't nobody want to do no reading game," said Layla, one of the young ladies from Mrs. Harper's class. "I wish my teacher was here. I'm tired of going to these other stupid classes."

A few of the other students chuckled. Hannah stopped herself from rolling her eyes because she and Layla had matching attitudes at the moment. She was so over the disrespect. She took a few deep breaths as she waited for the students' attention again.

"Sweetheart, I understand your frustration. Hopefully your teacher will be back tomorrow. Now, as I was saying, we are going to break up into teams and play a game. And those who *don't want* to participate can sit quietly and write a story or poem or read a book, but you will not disrupt this class anymore this period," Hannah said, trying to control her tone and voice level. "I'm not dealing with *anymore* foolishness today. Do I make myself clear?" she spoke between her teeth, eyeing Layla.

"Yeah," Layla mumbled, rolling her eyes.

"Great," Hannah said, fighting back her sarcasm. "I do have a little more candy in my desk for the winning team," she stated, trying to think of a way to keep this large group focused for the next few minutes.

"Oooh, candy. Bet. I'm ready to play," said Caleb, one of Hannah's students.

"You are so greedy," said Kaily, another one of her students.

"Alright, so listen up: As I break you all up, if you don't want to participate, come and sit in the seats here in the back or at the back table." She pointed to the section of the room she was indicating as a few of the students stood to move in that direction.

After setting up the teams, Hannah walked over to her portable desk in the corner near her larger desk and pulled up one of the Jeopardy reviews she had created a few days ago for her class. She then passed out her white boards and markers, assigned team captains, and moved her portable desk closer to the back. There was still no administrator, so Hannah abandoned trying to call again and hoped the students would get into this game.

Things were going well for about fifteen minutes until one of the boys from Mrs. Kingston's class gave the wrong answer and another boy started laughing.

"What's so funny?" the young man yelled, walking over to the other.

"You," the other boy stated.

"Alright, guys. Settle down. I already told you all I am not dealing with any more of this foolishness, so get it together, or you will be out in the hallway until someone comes. I'm over this nonsense,"

Hannah said, stepping between them. She felt the pulse in her neck thumping, and her head began to throb.

The one who had laughed stopped, but the other young man wouldn't, so Hannah asked the more aggressive one to move to the back near her desk.

The game continued, and everyone seemed to cooperate, but Hannah was already exhausted.

She wanted to get home to take a nap, but she knew that wasn't an option, having to pick up Ariel from daycare and cook dinner. As she anticipated the end of the school day, she prayed God would understand.

Lord there is so much on my plate now. I don't want to walk away from teaching. I really love what I do. Is it really time for me to leave? The truth was she was still afraid to take the leap.

Hannah heard the same two words she had heard over and over, but she couldn't imagine how she could pull it off at the moment. She continued to wait for the right time to move forward, and she had yet to move in the area of God's nudging, but she was simply afraid to do so. She felt unequipped and unprepared financially.

Trust me. The time is now. Obey now.

CHAPTER TWO

Wednesday, October 6

Despite her current dilemma, Hannah couldn't have asked for a greater blessing than motherhood, no matter how hard it could be at times. In addition to the craziness at school nowadays, being a mom was a nonstop additional career, but she wouldn't change it for the world. As she finished straightening up the living room before having to tuck in her daughter, Ariel, she couldn't help but think back over her life. All of her troubles seemed so far away now. Her life had been one roller coaster after another, and she was glad it was over—at least her life outside of school.

She and her husband, Levi, had struggled so long to get pregnant, not to mention the other disappointments that came along with it, but her dream had finally been realized. That's why she still couldn't understand why God was pressing her so much about opening a women's center. She was already serving the women at House of Hope Women's Shelter—she had been doing it for years. Hannah felt overwhelmed just thinking about what God couldn't understand. She had prayed. Well, maybe it was more like she was begging God to give her time, but he continued to press even more. His instructions had been a constant in her spirit.

Lord, you know Ariel is a handful at three, and I am still hosting my workshops with the women at the shelter on Zoom monthly. Can I at least get some credit for that? I just can't juggle anything else.

No matter how many times she gave God the same spiel, He continued to speak.

Hannah sighed. "Plus, I don't even have any experience in running a business with the responsibility of maintaining a building," she spoke into the air.

Trust me.

God continued to speak those same two words. She wanted to, but her plate was now running over, and there was still the issue of long-term funding. Fulfilling such a vision at this time was still as foggy as it was a year ago.

After finishing in the living room, Hannah turned off the lamp and set the alarm. She then headed up the hallway to Ariel's bedroom. Hannah pushed open the door, scanning the messy room she had cleaned not even thirty minutes ago. Ariel was over in the corner by the dresser attempting to put on the tutu Hannah had purchased a few days ago. Toys were scattered across the floor. Grinning and shaking her head, Hannah entered the room, nearly tripping over Ariel's doll in the middle of the floor.

The dim light from the ballerina lamp made the space feel inviting. The pink walls were accented with ballerina border all around, which matched Ariel's pink-and-white comforter, wall art, rug, and pillow set. Hannah couldn't stop admiring the little African American ballerina prints each time she entered her daughter's room. Her daughter had been drawn to ballerinas ever since she purchased the book *Zuri Learns to Stand On Her Toes* to read to her at bedtime, and she and Levi had enrolled Ariel in the Tiny Dancers Ballet Studio near Hannah's school. Ariel seemed to love it, and being around other toddlers was a plus. The daughter of April Evans, one of her friends, also attended the studio.

"Just what are you doing, little girl?" Hannah demanded to know, placing her hands on her hips.

"Mama, help me pull it down in the back. I want to wear my tutu," Ariel said.

Hannah's heart melted at the sound of her daughter's voice calling out *Mama*. She smiled as she scolded her. "Oh, no you don't. It is time for you to go to bed."

"I don't want to go to bed. I want to wear my tutu."

"No, ma'am. Come on. Let's put this away. I will help you put it on tomorrow."

"I'm not ready to go to bed, Mama."

"We are not doing this tonight, Ariel. Come on. Clean these toys up so we can read a bedtime story."

Suddenly, Ariel seemed to forget what she was doing, abandoned the tutu, and headed over to her bookshelf. "Mama, read my book, please."

She had grabbed *Zuri Learns to Stand On Her Toes* and was pulling at Hannah's arm.

"No, ma'am. Clean up these toys, then we will read the story."

"Okay," Ariel said, picking up one toy at a time.

At this rate, another hour will surely pass. Hannah chuckled and began assisting her daughter. When they were done, she instructed Ariel to climb in bed.

Hannah pulled the rocking chair with the same ballerina print covering it from the corner by the window and began reading. As she read each page and turned the book to reveal the pictures, Ariel gazed at them as if she was seeing them for the first time. At the end of the story, Hannah smiled at her little princess, stood, leaned in, and kissed her on the cheek.

"I love when you read my favorite story. You read it better than Daddy."

"*Awww.* Thank you, princess," Hannah said, remembering princess was also her dad's nickname for her.

"I love you, Mommy." Hannah's heart skipped a few beats at those words.

"I love you more, Busy Bee."

Once the story was over, Hannah grabbed Ariel's tiny hands and led her in prayer.

"Dear Lord, watch over Ariel as she sleeps. Keep and protect her from all hurt, harm, and danger.

Watch over me and Daddy, her nanas, her Pop Pop, her TT Brittany, Aunt Melissa, Uncle Joseph, and her Uncle Malik wherever he is." Hannah paused for a minute, thinking about her younger brother. She wondered why she and her sister had only heard from him a few times since he went away to the Marines.

Lord, I know he was hurt by Mama, but touch his heart to reach out and even come visit if he can. Help him to forgive Mama someday for mistreating me and for her years of drinking. She's a new woman today because of you, she prayed in her heart before continuing prayer with her daughter.

"Lord, help Ariel to grow into what you have created her to be. Help her to know your love as she walks through this life. Keep Mama and Daddy's health, so we will be here to raise her up in the way she should go. I pray that she will love you with all her heart. In Jesus' name. Amen."

"Amen. Thank you, Jesus," Ariel added, lifting her hands, rocking from side to side. Hannah chuckled. "Mama, read another story."

"No more stories, Ariel. Mama has to go to bed so I can get up for work, and you have to go to daycare in the morning."

"No, Mama. Another story, please," Ariel said, getting up and heading back over to her bookshelf to grab another book.

"No. Lay down. It's time to go to sleep, Ariel."

"Please, Mama," her daughter continued, poking out her bottom lip.

Hannah sighed, knowing she would be a part of team *No Sleep* if she couldn't get Ariel to bed soon. Levi was already knocked out, having to get up by 5:00 a.m., so it was all on her. She stood, walked over to the bookshelf, and grabbed another story to read to Ariel. Hannah grabbed a longer one this time, hoping it would do the trick. As she made her way back over to the rocking chair, she thought again about why this was not the ideal time to open a women's center. It would consume her time, and she needed to be with her daughter to help set the foundation for the rest of her life.

Lord, just not right now, Hannah said in her heart as she took a seat in the rocker, praying she would be able to get to sleep some time soon.

CHAPTER THREE

Friday, October 12

The following Friday, things were still chaotic at school. Hannah had finally made it to her short thirty-minute planning period. She sat at her desk with her head back and the lights out, grateful there were no meetings to attend. She contemplated resigning. *What is really going on in education? Things are getting crazier by the day.* In addition, she was sleep deprived because she and Levi had been up late with Ariel. Her daughter was running a low-grade fever, so she was at her mother-in-law's today. She was grateful for Mama Jefferson's support whenever they needed her. She'd texted to check on her daughter a few times already. Hannah was hoping it was just a little bug that would be over by the weekend.

A few times, she had heard a knock at the door, but she didn't answer, grateful her desk was not within view of the door's window. She was sure it was one of the other teachers wanting to talk. She just wasn't in the mood. To add to her stress, they had gone through yet another week of several teachers being out and her class periods being filled to capacity. The principal, Mrs. Sylvia Garrett, had even met with them on Tuesday about not switching classes going forward when there are so many teachers out. That wouldn't have bothered Hannah so much if she didn't have to deal with Jamal and hold difficult students in her room all day, even if they weren't on her roll.

Another irritation was that Mrs. Garrett was the third principal since Hannah had begun teaching at Rocklake Elementary nine years ago. She'd been blessed to remain at Rocklake the whole time since entering the field, but she didn't know how blessed she felt nowadays. Mrs. Garrett was the worse. Hannah's two former principals at least kept the school up, and the morale had never been so low. Rocklake had been known for academic achievement awards and so much more. *What happened?*

After their Tuesday meeting, Hannah had asked the principal if she could talk to her in private about her challenging student. She shared that his behavior was getting progressively worse, and it was causing the classroom environment to be unsafe for the other students. Hannah asked if she could have the behavior interventionist come and sit in her class to observe and assist with him. She didn't know what else to do. The parents were no help.

Mrs. Garrett had snapped and asked, "Do you think we are not supporting you? The behavior interventionist has to meet with several students. Mr. Ramsey can't just come and sit in your classroom all day. What strategies have you tried with Jamal yourself? Plus, you need to be focused more on the reading scores for the students in your two classes. They didn't do so great on the district Common Formative Assessment."

"Mrs. Garrett, many of our students came to us from fourth grade with low reading scores. I am doing my best to teach them the skills they are missing. They are slowly learning the fifth-grade skills," Hannah had explained.

"Well, there is going to have to be more done with attempting to grow these students."

Does this woman even care about her teachers? Hannah thought as she reflected on their conversation. *I'm trying to talk to her about a potentially dangerous situation, and she doesn't seem concerned at all. Lord, I swear you are trying to push me out, and you are doing a great job of it.*

Hannah didn't know what else to say to her unreasonable principal, so she had thanked her for her time and walked out of her office disgusted at the response she'd received. Attempting to shake off the unpleasant memory, Hannah asked in her heart again, *Lord, are you really trying to push me out?*

As she remained with her head back, rest didn't come because God had not stopped speaking to her heart about moving forward with the center for women. Hannah sighed. *Maybe I can expand beyond my Zoom meetings and start going into the shelter again and even a few churches to meet with women on Saturdays,* she thought, continuing to try to negotiate, but her shoulders tensed, knowing she just didn't have the time. Her weekends were busier now with her daughter's ballet, playdates, and finding alone time with her husband. They had more date nights in the past. Now, Ariel was the priority for them both.

With her time almost up, Hannah stood and passed out the interactive notebooks for her afternoon class, which she would be starting in a few minutes. They were finishing up crafting arguments. She always enjoyed coming up with creative topics for her students to debate. Today they were still working on writing the supporting details to back up their claim of whether or not they should be allowed to bring cell phones to school.

Hannah smiled as she thought about how passionate her students were about this topic. *Lord, there are some great things about teaching. Why does the other craziness have to drown out its joy?*

The time is now, she heard in her spirit for like the hundredth time, and it terrified her. Knowing she was slowly losing her own debate with the Lord, Hannah finished up in silence and headed out to grab her group from specials, her stress levels rising as she worried about how eventually stepping out of the classroom would look.

As soon as she entered the hallway, she ran into one of the fifth-grade teachers.

"Oh, you were in there. I wanted to ask you how you planned to teach the plot elements standard next week," Mr. Rutherford said.

Still not wanting to talk and doing her best not to be rude to her coworker, Hannah quickly responded, "I found two short stories I'm going to use. We'll walk through the first one together, and they will read the other on their own and plot the story with a partner." Then, she attempted to go around him.

"Sounds good. Can you share the stories with me in an email?"

"Sure. I'll do it before leaving today," Hannah replied, moving quickly up the hallway. She knew he meant well, but her mind was consumed at the moment.

"Great. Thanks. And by the way, are you okay? You have been looking a little stressed," he continued.

Hannah drew in a deep breath and turned back towards him, "I'm okay, I guess."

Hannah liked her teammate. He was in his late thirties, a little older than her. She felt comfortable talking to him, but at the moment, she wanted to be left alone. It was nothing against him. Plus, she didn't feel comfortable sharing anything personal with him. Although he was fairly young, he would often share great wisdom with her and the other fifth-grade teachers.

"Try to keep your head up, and if you have to take a day, do it. Self-care is the best care."

"Thanks for that encouragement, but I don't think that is the solution for me. I have to grab my students now."

"No problem. So do I."

As Hannah walked away, more and more frustration rose within her. She wanted to continue trusting God who had loved and healed her more than she could effectively describe, but she just didn't know about this water-walking faith that God was asking her to step out on.

CHAPTER FOUR

Saturday, October 13

The weekend arriving was like a gentle rain after a long drought. Hannah needed it to remain for an extended time. She'd never felt so drained and unsure about what she should do about the pressing from God. After time in prayer, preparing and eating breakfast with her husband and daughter, she decided to get out of the house for a bit and go to see her long-time mentor, Ms. Priscilla.

Levi had agreed to take care of their little busy bee, Ariel.

Ms. Priscilla had led her to Christ and had played a significant role in Hannah's life for years. She hadn't seen nor had the chance to hang out with her in weeks, and she didn't know when she would get the chance again. Things had been so hectic at school, continuing the So That You May Live ministry workshops, and since becoming a mom, she'd hardly had any time for anyone else in her close-knit circle of friends and family. She felt horrible because they used to get together often, but they hadn't as much lately.

Hannah dialed Ms. Priscilla's cell phone number to let her know she was stopping by the shop. A few minutes later, Hannah pulled into the parking lot of the small strip mall on Ray Mills Road, about fifteen minutes from House of Hope Women's Shelter. She had hosted her mentoring workshops there in person for some time. Then, after giving birth to Ariel, she had begun hosting monthly Zoom workshops with most of the same group of women who had attended in person. Hannah had made new connections as some of the women had moved on and gotten jobs and places to live, which she was proud of. Their next meeting was next Saturday morning.

Ms. Priscilla had relocated a few months ago when she couldn't maintain the payments at the other shop where she had been for years due to the raised rent prices. Everything had become more expensive, not just in Forest Park, but all across Georgia. Hannah shook her head. That was why Ms. Priscilla was still working at age sixty-six. She had asked her recently when she thought she would be able to retire. Ms. Priscilla said she would at some point, but for now she only worked a few days a week, which gave her more time to rest and relax. She told Hannah what she always did, "When God tells me it's time, I will shut down completely." Hannah knew her mentor's staying was her trying to reach more people with the gospel. That's what she adored about her. Mrs. Priscilla's faith was one she always admired.

Not only did Hannah need to get Ms. Priscilla's advice about walking away from the classroom, she was also in need of a big hug from her. She always seemed to know the right words to say to help Hannah put things in the right perspective, so she turned off the engine, grabbed her purse, and made her way to the front door.

Opening the door to the shop, Hannah was reminded of how small this new space really was with the other stylist and her two clients sitting and waiting. The space was so compact that it had just enough room for the two styling areas, the wash sink, and the small waiting area.

Walking over to Ms. Priscilla's chair, Hannah smiled at her mentor, noting her hair had grayed a little more, and her eyes seemed to hold more wrinkles than the last time she'd seen her. *She looks a little older. Maybe I'm exaggerating*, Hannah thought. Ms. Priscilla stopped curling her client's hair for a moment and stepped from behind her chair to give Hannah a big hug.

"How are you, sweetness?"

"I'm doing okay. How about you?"

"I'm doing amazing. God is still good."

"I'm so glad to see you," Hannah said.

"Same to you. I'll be done with this customer in just a few, then we can go next door, grab a bowl of homemade soup, and catch up."

"Sounds good. I'll sit over here and wait," Hannah said, pointing to the only empty chair remaining in the narrow waiting area.

Hannah took a seat on the worn metal chair, watching as Ms. Priscilla finished a middle-aged woman's hair. She styled the woman's hair into a neck-length bob and curled it into spirals. Hannah thought it was cute on her, but it wouldn't be a style she would wear. Ms. Priscilla was gifted though. Not only did they attend the same church, she had also been Hannah's beautician for years. Since transitioning to natural, Hannah didn't come as often, only to have her hair trimmed or when she wanted a silk press, which was coming up soon. Hannah rubbed her fingers through her roots, making a mental note to schedule an appointment with Ms. Priscilla before leaving.

After the client paid and left, Hannah helped Ms. Priscilla clean her area. She grabbed the broom and swept up the excess hair around the chair while Ms. Priscilla sanitized and wiped down everything. Then, they both washed their hands in the tiny restroom and headed next door to the small mom-and-pop diner, Homestyle Haven.

"Oh, I forgot. I need to schedule an appointment for a trimming and silk press."

"Just text me a good time when you get a moment, and I will fit you in."

"Okay."

Once inside, they chatted for a few minutes as they waited for their food. "Ms. Priscilla, this looks and smells amazing," Hannah said, grabbing her bowl carefully from the counter. They headed over to a booth in the back corner. She had only been there a few times, but she had never tried their soup, only their salads and sandwiches, which were amazing.

"I love this place," Ms. Priscilla replied, placing her soup in front of her before sitting.

They then joined hands to pray. After Ms. Priscilla led them in prayer, Hannah scooped a teaspoon of the steaming chicken and dumpling soup, blowing it before eating the contents on the spoon. She and Ms. Priscilla sat in silence for a few minutes, enjoying their soup. Ms. Priscilla broke the silence by asking Hannah how things were going.

Hannah took a deep breath before responding, "Things are hectic at school, and I have been hearing God say it's time for me to step out and open the center."

"Well? What are you planning to do?"

"That's one of the things I wanted to talk with you about. I really don't want to walk away, but I feel God is pushing me out, and I still don't feel prepared at all to leave."

Ms. Priscilla remained silent for several moments before speaking. Hannah wondered if she was praying.

"Well, sweetness, God can allow things to get our attention. Is He pushing you out? I don't think so because He gave us a free will. Is He nudging you? Probably. He has a great work for you to do."

"Ms. Priscilla, I still don't think I'm ready to take such a huge step, but I'm torn. Not only do I love teaching, it is also a consistent salary for me."

"Well, it sounds like you have to make a decision."

"Huh?"

"God has already spoken, Hannah. Now he needs a response from you. You have put God's vision off for long enough."

"It's not that easy, Ms. Priscilla. I still haven't heard anything about more funding, so there are still not enough funds to step out there. I did reach out about interns and volunteers, but I haven't gotten a lot of response. I guess most of them are just not interested in not getting paid, and I can't blame them. Plus, I still don't know much about being a business owner and being responsible for a building and the overhead that comes with it. What if it doesn't work out, and I have given up my steady income? That would put so much stress on our household. Not to mention, being a mother of a toddler isn't the easiest job."

"What if it doesn't? Isn't that God's job to worry about the details? Are you willing to trust Him?"

Hannah paused a long moment before responding, "I mean, I do trust Him, but that's a huge step."

"So, you trust Him only when you can understand things? Is that right?"

"*Ummm,* no, well…I guess."

"Sweetness, you know I only give it to you straight. To put it plain, you are disobeying God's instructions. The God we serve doesn't give us small visions. They are always going to be bigger than we are because it is the Lord who will get the glory in our lives. So, if He is going to get the glory, of course it won't be easy because we have to trust Him every step of the way."

"I hear you. I do plan to obey, just not right now. I don't need to remind you about the cost of living. Even though Levi says he's got me, I want to help and not become a burden on him."

"Delayed obedience is still disobedience. It sounds like God has already moved on your husband's heart. He is just waiting on you to move in his instructions," Ms. Priscilla said, patting the top of Hannah's hand.

"It's just so much to think about right now."

"You know I love you, but I have to tell you what thus says the Lord."

"I know. It is just so stressful."

"I understand, but we still have to trust that the Lord will make a way. Why would He give you a vision if He wasn't planning on making a way for it to come to pass? You have to trust Him."

"I really thought I was."

"That's why we all need Jesus. Only He knows what we need, not us. Once you have walked through this next level of faith, you can share that testimony with the women you encounter. There will be someone who is struggling with that very thing. That's how God works. Trust God for the manna. He knows how much funding you have and how much you will need. He also knows what your household needs. He will bring the provision. It will all work out. It begins when you obey Him, by moving in His instructions, not searching for a way for you to fix and solve things. You don't need to see the whole picture. He does. Release control to Christ."

"But this is so hard," Hannah said.

"God's got you, sweetness," Ms. Priscilla stated. You don't have to unfold all your plans for the center all at once. Take it one step at a time. It will be a process. I have seen God move numerous times in my business. He has never failed me. You know God as a miracle worker. Think about what He did in your life giving you and Levi that beautiful little girl. Watch Him do it again."

"I know, and I hate feeling like I have very little faith after that experience. I thank God for you. You keep reminding me, if He did it then, He will do it again."

"That's right. He didn't somehow change since He opened your womb," Ms. Priscilla said, lifting her hands and giving God a praise. "Lord, you are a good God."

"Amen," Hannah said.

"Now, as far as the funding, have you tried reaching out to more churches or angel investors and venture capital firms? You should've learned about that in one of those business classes you've taken."

"I did, and a friend I met at one of the meetups hosted for faith-based organizations, Dr. Taylor, has helped me locate and apply for a few of those."

"Good. Sweetness, walk in obedience. Stop trying to figure it out. God's got you. You can trust in His power, provision, strength, and direction."

Hannah looked up from her soup at Ms. Priscilla. "Okay."

"Choose to obey Him now."

"I'm just so afraid of failing or moving too quickly."

"God charged me as your mentor. Just like when I helped you begin mentoring the women at the shelter, I will help you see this through. So, no matter who else is assisting you, I'm bringing up the rear so God will be well pleased. I will keep you in prayer. Remember, obedience is better than sacrifice."

"I know. Please keep me in prayer against the fear and self-doubt I'm struggling with. I have probably said this a million times: You have been a true Godsend in my life. Thank you for everything. You always give it to me straight, even when I want you to take my side."

"You are most welcome, sweetness. You have become like a daughter to me, and don't you worry, I've already been praying for you," Ms. Priscilla said, squeezing Hannah's hand.

"Thank you so much."

"And I will be praying for you to take God's hand and release the hand of fear. The L.I.V.E. vision is not only for the women you will minister to, but it is also for you. God wants you to L.I.V.E. and He wants to use you to help other women to do the same," Ms. Priscilla said, referring to how Hannah should Learn about Christ, Improve her view of herself, find her Voice, and Empower other women to do the same.

Hannah smiled at her mentor, noting how she had memorized the acronym. She then nodded, "Thanks again. I appreciate you. You don't know how much."

After texting Levi and letting him know that she should be home by 2:30, Hannah chatted with her mentor for another hour, long after they had finished their soup. She was grateful for this woman. She had taught her so much about Christ and how she had been created for His purpose. Ms. Priscilla didn't care about Hannah getting offended at her words. She wanted her to be free in Christ and to walk in what He had instructed, so she was grateful for all she'd shared with her. She knew it was easier said than done, but nothing she had walked through in her life had been easy. God never said it would be, but she did have the support she needed to press on and to take the big leap of faith. She knew Ms. Priscilla was right. It was possible with God. He hadn't failed her in the past. Why would He now?

Lord, help me to obey and walk in the fullness of what you have called me to do. Deliver me from all fear.

CHAPTER FIVE

Monday, October 28

Two weeks later, Hannah's school day started off on a positive note. All of the fifth-grade teachers were present, which was the first time in weeks, so she didn't have any extra students in her room.

This is a welcomed relief, Hannah thought.

Hannah's enrichment/remediation group went well. The students seemed to enjoy practicing the central idea with the digital cards she'd purchased last year. The other students worked well in partners while Hannah and Mrs. McNair, the reading intervention teacher, worked with their small groups. As the hour came to a close, Ms. McNair closed out and sent her group back to their seats to work on the central idea seatwork. She monitored the other students while Hannah finished up with her group.

After Hannah dismissed her students back to their seats, Mrs. McNair headed to her next class. A few minutes later, Amir, the class comedian, began making jokes with a few of the other boys about how he'd beat them in Fortnite over the weekend. He then walked toward Jamal's desk stating, "I beat you too, kid. You almost beat me, but I came back."

"You didn't beat nobody," Jamal said.

"I did beat you. Stop capping."

Knowing Jamal's temperament, Hannah walked over to intervene, instructing Amir to go to his seat.

Amir complied and hurried over, sat down, and started cracking jokes with Kaily. If Hannah hadn't known any better, she would have sworn Kaily and Amir were siblings. They had such a love-hate relationship.

Hannah walked over to her portable desk and switched the screen to the social studies lesson slide, which included their opener. The students had to match the country with the description. Most of the class had taken out their notebooks. She reminded the others to take out theirs and get started. As Hannah walked around observing the answers the students came up with, she noticed Jamal getting up and walking over to Amir's desk.

"Jamal, take a seat, please," Hannah said.

He didn't move. He stood there glaring at Amir. Never taking much seriously, Amir began laughing, "Man what's wrong with you?"

"You," Jamal replied.

Taking in a breath, Hannah prayed there would be no incident with Jamal today. She made her way across the room toward the boys. That's when Jamal pushed Amir, but because Amir was slightly heavier and taller, he didn't budge. Amir laughed even more. "Man it's not that serious. I was just playing around."

"Alright, Jamal, remember we don't put our hands on our classmates. Go ahead and have a seat."

"No," he screamed.

"Jamal, you have to sit down, or let's step into the hallway so you can take a cool down."

"I said no."

After the second no, Hannah stood between Jamal and Amir, so Jamal wouldn't hit him. As she stood there, she attempted to talk with

Jamal in a low tone. "You seem like you're having a bad day. Would you like to go see the counselor, or maybe you can take a breather in another classroom?" Hannah asked.

There was no response. He just continued to glare at Amir.

"Look, I'm sorry, man. Okay. I was only joking around," Amir said, but Jamal didn't budge.

"Okay, Jamal. We have to get started with the social studies lesson. You have to calm down, or you may have to go sit in the office."

At those words, Jamal walked back over near his desk. He stood beside it for a moment. Then he sat down. Hannah was relieved nothing more transpired. She walked back over to pull her portable desk to the front of the room and walked around again to see who had finished the opener. The next thing she knew, Jamal was heading over to the reading corner. He grabbed her wooden stool, which the students used when they sat over there, and headed back toward where the rest of the class sat. Hannah's eyes widened when he lifted it over his head.

"What are you doing, Jamal? Put that stool down."

"No," he replied as he walked closer to where she stood. "You won't send me to the office. Send him," he screamed, turning toward Amir, the stool still over his head.

He had a wild look in his eyes, so Hannah walked over to block his view of Amir. "Jamal, look at me. You need to go put that stool down."

"I said no."

Needing some assistance, Hannah turned and pressed the call button on the wall a few steps away from her, but she kept her eyes on Jamal. It called into the front office. As she released the button, the stool came flying toward her, smashing into her left elbow as she attempted to block it from hitting her in the face. The ringing into the office continued until Mrs. Jennings, the front office clerk, came through the loudspeaker in the center of the classroom ceiling.

"How may I help you?"

The other students were yelling at Jamal for what he had done, and Hannah was doubled over in pain, her arm throbbing, "I need an administrator right away," Hannah yelled over the noise, grimacing.

"Is this Mrs. Jefferson?"

"Yes. I've been hit."

"Oh....okay. Calling someone right now."

After Mrs. Jennings clicked off the loudspeaker, Hannah had just enough strength to open the classroom door and push the stool out into the hallway as she continued to keep her eyes on Jamal, who just stood there glaring at her. She then told Kaily to go get Mr. Rutherford, one of the other fifth-grade teachers. The girl looked terrified.

Hannah waved her out of the room with her right arm and stood between Jamal and the other students. They were still yelling at him, and a few of the girls were crying.

"Guys and ladies, it will be okay. Please try to relax."

Hannah prayed for God to give her wisdom in this situation. Jamal was a ticking time bomb that had exploded. Just then, Mr. Rutherford rushed into the room with Kaily behind him. He hurried over to Hannah.

"Mrs. Jefferson, are you okay?"

"No. I was hit with a stool."

"Hit? What? Who?"

"This young man here," Hannah said, pointing to Jamal who now sat in the reading corner on the piece of carpet, staring at the floor.

"Did you call the off—"

"Yes, Mrs. Jefferson. You needed assistance?" Mrs. Garrett, the principal, asked rushing into the room.

"Yes. I was hit with a stool," Hannah explained, trying to control her tone as she thought about her attempt to get help for the same student just last week. Her arm was throbbing. She blinked back tears.

"Oh, no. Are you in pain?" Mrs. Garrett asked.

What do you think? Hannah thought, growing more annoyed. "Yes. It hurts pretty bad."

"Well, let's get you to the office for the nurse to look at it. Mr. Rutherford, do you mind taking her students into your room while I see who can cover?"

"Sure. No problem," he said, instructing the students to grab their chairs and come across the hall to his room.

"And Jamal, you come with me," the principal continued.

As they headed down the hallway to the front office, Hannah could overhear the questions Mrs. Garrett asked Jamal, as if somehow Hannah had made him throw the stool and hit her.

"What did Mrs. Jefferson do to stop Amir from making fun of you?"

"Did she tell Amir she would send him to the office too?"

Lord, I can't believe this woman. Why is she like this? Hannah wondered.

Meanwhile, Jamal was responding the same way to Mrs. Garrett as he had inside the room. She attempted to shush him as he screamed at her, seeming annoyed by her continued questions about the incident.

Once inside the office, the principal instructed Jamal to sit up front and not to move for any reason. He refused, poked out his lips, balled up his fist, and stood next to the chair she instructed him to sit in. She shook her head and turned away from him. She then turned and asked to see Hannah after the nurse checked her out. Hannah nodded and headed toward the nurse's office at the end of the hallway.

After filling out an incident report as much as she could and being given workman's comp paperwork, Nurse Valentine, an older woman in her sixties, examined Hannah's arm, she cried out in pain. Nurse Valentine informed Hannah that her arm was swollen, and she needed to get it checked out at the ER. She gave her an ice pack, which only soothed the pain a little. Hannah was grateful it wasn't her right arm, the one she did everything with. She asked the nurse if she could use her office phone to call her husband. Levi picked up on the second ring.

"Hello," Levi said, sounding confused. "Babe, is everything okay? Why are you calling me from the school phone? Where's your cell phone?"

"Hey. I was hit with a stool."

"Wait. What?"

"Yes, you heard me correctly."

"What do you mean you were hit? Who hit you?"

"One of my students."

"You are joking, right?"

"No, I'm not."

"I'm on my way up there. They are going to have to explain to me how they allowed this to happen."

"No, Levi. It's okay."

"Hannah, this is not okay. I need to have a conversation with that principal."

"No. Let me handle it."

"I want to handle it. Was it that same li'l joker that you went to her about?"

"Yes."

"These people have lost their minds."

"Levi, I got it. The nurse did say I need to go to the ER. Can you come and take me?"

"Of course. I'm on my way, and I need to have a little talk with Jesus before I get there."

"Please behave when you get here."

"I'll try," her husband replied, sounding angry.

"Levi, just let me handle it."

"Okay, babe. I'll be there in a few. I love you."

"I love you too."

After hanging up with Levi, Hannah headed up the hall to the principal's office. She shook her head when she looked up and noticed Jamal was still standing, now with his arms crossed. He turned away when he noticed her looking at him. Hannah didn't feel up to talking to Mrs. Garrett again. She just knew the woman would say something to frustrate her even further, but she had to wait until Levi got there anyway, so she might as well meet with her as the principal had requested. Standing at the door, she lifted her right arm and knocked on the closed door with all of the positive quotes around the door frame. Hannah rolled her eyes. Mrs. Garrett instructed her to enter.

"Hello, Mrs. Jefferson. What did the nurse tell you?"

"She said I need to have it looked at," Hannah replied, remaining in the doorway. "My husband is on the way to take me to the ER."

"Oh, wow. I'm so sorry that happened to you."

Are you really sorry? Hannah wondered, not in the mood to be fake.

"Have a seat. I just wanted to find out what happened."

Hannah moved slowly to the first leather chair in front of Mrs. Garrett's desk, hoping this would be over soon. She began explaining what transpired in the classroom before Jamal threw the stool. As she shared, Hannah could sense that what Ms. Garrett was about to say was going to infuriate her. The woman clearly didn't have her best interest at heart.

"So, did you correct Amir when he was teasing him?"

"Yes, I did speak to Amir. As a matter of fact, he apologized to Jamal."

"Hmmmm." Mrs. Garrett grunted.

"Will Jamal receive a consequence for throwing the stool?" Hannah asked.

"Yes. He will receive in-school suspension for three days."

"Excuse me?" Hannah asked, heat rushing to her face.

"What's the problem?" Mrs. Garrett asked, shifting to the other side of her chair, staring at Hannah.

"You don't think there's a problem with only giving him in-school suspension?" Hannah asked, matching her principal's stare, her anger rising.

"He has never really been in trouble before, and I want to have the counselor speak to him about his anger."

"I already talked to you about this, and you brushed me off. I have attempted to call the parents numerous times, and I had the counselor speak to him already."

"Excuse me, Mrs. Jefferson. I didn't brush you off. I simply told you that the behavior interventionist had a list of students he needed to meet with," Mrs. Garrett said, raising her voice.

Completely annoyed now, Hannah asked, "Mrs. Garrett, how do you not give out-of-school suspension to an angry student who has hit a teacher, not with an eraser or a piece of paper, but a wooden stool? And this student has hit other students and been noncompliant more than I can count. How does he not receive a harsher consequence?"

"Mrs. Jefferson, I understand you are upset, but many of our students are experiencing some difficulties in their lives."

"I understand that, but it is not okay for them to throw things and hit teachers, and I could have been knocked out if that stool would have hit me in my head. I blocked it with my arm. Would he have a different consequence if he had hit you?"

"Mrs. Jefferson, I don't see where that question is relevant."

"I don't see how you don't find it relevant, Mrs. Garrett. I don't mean any disrespect, but I don't feel supported."

"I fully support you, Mrs. Jefferson."

"Can he just be moved to a different classroom?"

"Well, we could, but we would have to try to get his parents in here and explain that you, the teacher, are requesting to have him moved. Again, I'm sorry, Mrs. Jeffe—"

"Mrs. Garrett, I don't think I can take much more of this. I have never experienced anything like this. I could have been seriously injured, and you don't seem to care, and you are doing your best to blame me. I don't know if I'm going to return in January. I don't want to leave, but you are leaving me no other choice. This is just too much. All I'm asking for is your support. I care about Jamal and his wellbeing. That's why I came to you for help, but you're blaming me for his actions, and it's not right."

"Put it in writing," Ms. Garrett finally said, slamming her hand on her desk, seeming annoyed after Hannah's previous statement.

"Excuse me?" Hannah asked, confused.

"You said you don't think you are returning for the second semester. Put it in writing," her principal repeated.

Really?

After those words, Mrs. Garrett turned toward her computer in the corner and began typing something. With her back still turned to Hannah, she then said, "You can go get checked out now. I have someone covering your class."

Hannah wasn't surprised but disappointed. This changed everything for her. She didn't really want to resign, but she couldn't put her life on the line. That would be exactly what she was doing if she remained at Rocklake any longer than needed. She knew it wasn't just here. She'd seen and heard from teacher after teacher with similar issues. The landscape of the world of education had changed, and she had to move on. Her heart ached because of her love for it, but it was out of her control.

At that moment, Ms. Priscilla's words came back to her: *Obedience is better than sacrifice.*

CHAPTER SIX

Saturday, November 2

Having taken off the rest of the week and not returning until the following Wednesday to allow her arm to heal and to have a mental break from school, Hannah was enjoying her Saturday despite the pain and swelling in her arm. The doctor had informed her that there was nothing broken. It was sprained. It was wrapped in Ace bandage from her shoulder to just below her elbow, and she had been prescribed eight hundred milligrams of ibuprofen for the pain. She had to laugh to keep from screaming, still unable to believe what had transpired with Jamal.

However, she felt the incident with Jamal had sealed the deal for her. She didn't even want to return next Wednesday, not to mention in January, but she didn't want to cause any problems with her teaching license by not doing things properly. Hannah had prayed for God to give her clear direction, as if He hadn't already. She was still terrified to take the entrepreneurial leap, so when she wasn't in pain, she had spent some time looking for curriculum writing positions outside of the field of education to be a cushion for her once she left, just in case. She was still struggling a little with the fear of the unknown. Ms. Priscilla's words had plagued her mind for days. After checking her business PayPal account yesterday, she'd learned she'd received more donations through social media and her website. She'd also received a few small grants. She technically had enough to open as she waited to hear about the other grants. Hannah had met with the board again two weeks ago to review her plans. Pastor Dickerson and Pastor Gibson had remained in contact with Hannah. They wanted to see her walk fully in God's will. They both echoed her long-time mentor's words, *Delayed obedience is still disobedience.* She knew it was all in love.

Hannah didn't know what she was so afraid of, especially since Jamal would be back in her room still throwing things and still hitting and threatening the other students in her class in a few days. Yes, this was a battle she couldn't win. She was over it—not being able to reach Jamal's parents and having to try to teach and manage the child's behavior at the same time, the teachers being out all the time and not knowing when she would have to deal with Jamal and having wall-to-wall students, and not to mention the useless *strategies* she'd tried with him. In addition, she didn't want to have to bail her husband out of jail for showing out at the school. He was not happy, and neither was she, yet she still had a few more weeks to deal with it. She knew funding and sustaining a center was nothing to God.

I have to walk away.

Over the past few days, Levi had been trying to encourage her that the stress of the classroom would be over soon. He had agreed with her decision not to return in January. He supported her one hundred percent and didn't seem to be worried about the possible impact on their household, but she hadn't told him that she wavered with resigning. Hannah was embarrassed at how her faith seemed to shift so much, even after seeing the hand of God move in her life more than once.

Lord, I'm sorry. I don't want to doubt.

Free from pain after taking her meds once she had eaten a bowl of cereal about thirty minutes ago, Hannah now sat at the kitchen table finishing up her cup of coffee in silence. Levi and Ariel were still asleep. She enjoyed her quiet time from 5:30 until about 7:00 before breakfast every Saturday. She picked up her cell phone and opened her Bible app. It always gave her a verse of the day. Hannah did a double take when she noticed Joshua 1:9. *Have I not commanded you? Be strong and courageous. Do not be frightened, and do not be dismayed, for the LORD your God is with you wherever you go.* Hannah read the scripture two more times. God was definitely speaking to her. She felt he was letting her know that he was with her, in the classroom or outside of it. Hannah was grateful for his grace. She said another prayer of repentance, feeling awful about her lack of trust. God led her to read Joshua chapters one and two. She then stood and headed into her home office to grab her journal.

Hannah returned to the kitchen, sat down, and made a list of God's instructions to Joshua and how he'd responded. She then wrote out practical ways she could practice obeying God as Joshua had. Laying down her journaling pen, Hannah bowed her head and prayed. *Lord, I have to admit, this is a lot for me. Joshua seemed to be a fearless leader. He seemed to obey you without a doubt. Please help me to get to that place. I want to serve women as you have used me with those at House of Hope Women's Shelter, but I know this is bigger than that. It's about reaching more women. I honestly think I'm too young. I'm only thirty-one years old. Many of the women I help will more than likely be older than me. I don't feel prepared, and I fear failure. Lead me and guide me. Help me to be obedient and not rebellious, in Jesus' name. Amen.*

After her prayer, Hannah sat quietly for a few minutes. She heard in her spirit, *Like Joshua, I want to use you to lead the women out of captivity, into the promise I have for them.*

Hannah replied, *Lord, I don't know why you chose me, but help me to release control and allow you to use me for your glory.*

Hannah then wrote the L.I.V.E. acronym at the bottom of her notes as a reminder of the vision, *I will help women to L.I.V.E. They will <u>learn</u> about Christ so they can understand who they really are, use what they've learned to <u>improve</u> their view of themselves, find their <u>voice</u>, and <u>empower</u> other women to do the same.* After rereading the acronym

God had given her recently as the vision for the organization, she reflected on how God seemed to be walking her personally through each part as well. Hannah placed her gel pen in the center of that page and closed her journal. Then, she headed back into the office. She was grateful for their renovated ranch style three-bedroom home. They had sold their townhome after Ariel was born because they wanted more space but didn't want to spend a fortune. Now she didn't have to run up and down the stairs when she needed something, and the 2,200 square footage was plenty of space for their daughter to run around in. Not to mention, their spacious backyard where Levi had set up a small swing with a slide for Ariel, which was one of Hannah's favorite places to hang out and journal.

Entering the office, she placed her journal on her favorite oversized chair and grabbed her laptop. Hannah felt led to do something now to show she was willing to obey God. No more excuses. Once she made it back into the kitchen, Hannah pulled her chair back up to their wooden table. She logged into her school email. She would put in her resignation and allow God to lead her down the path He desired for her. As she slowly typed in her username and password with her right arm and grabbed the security code from her phone, she was reminded again of how she didn't want to be put in a situation like this again. Her arm could have been broken.

She repented again, asking God to help her to be courageous in Christ. Taking a deep breath, Hannah pulled up her school email. It took her some time to type out her resignation, and her heart pounded at each word. She paused for a moment, clenching the cross charm around her neck as if it would cease her fears. Hannah continued the email, asking God to give her the words. Finally done, she read it a few times before hitting the send button. Although the whole process seemed terrifying, a surprise feeling came over Hannah—relief. It was a peace she hadn't felt since accepting Christ as her personal savior five years ago.

After logging out of her school email, she checked her personal email for any messages about the larger grants she'd applied for. There was nothing there. Determined to keep the faith, she decided to do a search for an affordable building to lease anyway. First, she texted Ms. Priscilla to tell her about the step she'd taken. Hannah added hearts and praying hands. Ms. Priscilla replied with the words, *Trust Him. Watch Him move.* Hannah nodded and smiled as if Ms. Priscilla could see her. She then took a bold step. She opened her search engine and began looking up small commercial buildings in their area.

Nope, that is way too expensive. Oh, Lord that one costs even more, she thought as she searched. Then, she came across a small space a few miles from the shelter. "That isn't as close as I would have wished, but it might work," Hannah said out loud, typing the phone number and address into the notes app in her cell phone. She would go check it out. "Plus, it's a good price," she said out loud to herself as she viewed the images.

"What's a good price?" Levi asked, entering the kitchen. Hannah jumped, her heart racing again.

"Man, you scared me."

"Sorry, babe. Good morning," Levi said, kissing Hannah on the forehead. "As I was saying, what's a good price?"

"This building. I was looking around for a space to open the So That You May Live Women's Center. Look at it," Hannah said, turning the computer screen toward her husband.

"It's kind of old, but it could be a start."

"It doesn't look too bad, right?" Hannah asked.

"So, you have made up your mind to obey the Lord?"

"Yes." Hannah smiled at her husband. "I put in my resignation a few minutes ago."

"Seriously?" Levi asked, attempting to do the moonwalk, his chocolate bald head shining beneath the bright kitchen lights reminded Hannah of a Milk Dud. "Now I don't have to go to jail."

"Stop playing. Your daughter and I need you out in these free streets. But yes, I felt God speaking more to me this morning, and Ms. Priscilla's words about obedience have been plaguing my mind since I talked to her, so I decided to step out on the ocean like Peter. Or maybe it's a small lake or just a water puddle," Hannah said.

"Really? A water puddle? No, babe, this is huge. Some people never move their feet at all out of fear."

"*Ummm,* I am scared, but I did it afraid."

"And God will honor your small faith step. Oh, come on. Keep walking, Peter," Levi said.

Hannah loved her some him. "Do you really support me on this?" she asked.

"Of course. Hasn't the Lord brought us through many times? And, if He told you to do this, He will make provisions. Don't worry so much. He's got us. We will have to cut back on spending and eating out, but I believe He will make a way once again."

"You're always my biggest cheerleader."

"Am I not supposed to be?"

"*Awww.* That's my man."

"But you know your greatest cheerleader and provider is Christ."

"Point taken."

"By the way, is Ariel still sleeping? She is really quiet," Hannah said.

"No. She's back there watching cartoons, propped up on her pillow like she's grown."

"I swear she is an old soul," Hannah said. "We can get her up in a few minutes after we make breakfast."

"No. You relax. I'll make breakfast. I'm ready for some grub," Levi said, patting his flat stomach.

"Uh, no. You know you can't make grits," Hannah said. "You make the bacon and eggs. I'll handle the grits. I have use of one of my arms."

"Oh, that's cold. How you gone do a brotha like that?" Levi asked, grinning.

"I love you. When you love someone, you tell them the truth."

"Wow. Are you sure you love me?"

"I am. Now, step aside so I can grab the grit pot," Hannah said, brushing passed her husband and laughing.

"Alright. Let's get these pots boiling and sizzling with some grits, eggs, and bacon," Levi said, walking over to the other cabinet and pulling the frying pan from beneath it. He then began dancing again after she asked him to grab the grits and the butter from the refrigerator. "Yes, Lord. A brotha is about to eat good!"

"You love stuffing your gut."

"Facts," Levi said, still dancing as he put the bacon in the pan.

"That stomach won't always be flat," said Hannah, giggling and resting her hand on his belly.

"Oh, you got jokes. That's what exercise is for. A brotha will not be deprived from the grub. Eating is a necessity."

They both shared a laugh as her husband pulled her into an embrace. She enjoyed when they cooked together and spent time laughing and talking. He never ceased to amaze her. She had to admit she was surprised at his response to her actually putting in her resignation. She prayed he would remain this way, through the process of opening and running the center. He had been a true blessing throughout their eight years of marriage. Taking the pot from him, Hannah thanked God for sending him into her life. With God, his support, and the support of the others, maybe, just maybe, everything would work out. No, it would work out. It was time for her to speak it and believe it with her whole heart, so after breakfast, Hannah continued to move by faith and work on a plan to open up. She figured she would be ready once the funding finally came in.

Her cell phone pinged. Hannah looked down and saw her sister, Brittany's name pop up. She was sending her a text. She would read it a little later. She continued working, and a few minutes later, her phone pinged again. Hannah glanced at her phone again and saw that it was another message from Brittany, so she decided to go ahead and read them.

Hey, sis. Call me when you get a chance. Did you know Aunt Loretta is now at Mama's? She has been there for about a week now because Malcolm began threatening her when she filed for a divorce.

He refused to leave the house. This is a mess. I didn't want to upset you, but I thought you should know in case he tries to show up at Mama's while you're there.

Hannah sat back in her office chair and read the message again. Anger rose in her heart as she read the message a third time before clicking out of the app. *Why is she there? Why is she so close? Why is this happening now? If that husband of hers comes anywhere near me...* Hannah screamed inside, standing and pacing. *Haven't I dealt with enough? Why did it even take Aunt Loretta so long to leave him? That's what she gets,* Hannah fumed. *I don't need this right now, Lord. I've obeyed You. I took the step of faith You instructed.*

Hannah and her aunt had been estranged for years. She was cordial the few times she had gone around her when her mom visited or when her mom was on the phone with her, but that was as far as things went between the two of them due to her past experience with her aunt and her awful husband.

Lord, is this a cruel joke?

You must fully forgive so I can use you to change the lives of the women I'm sending.

Hannah froze at those words. "Lord, I forgave them, but do I have to be around either of them? And do I have to be around someone who hurt me so bad? That man is disgusting. And isn't opening a center enough stress for me right now? Haven't I dealt with enough?" She spoke into the air.

You must fully forgive them both, she heard in her spirit again.

Hannah didn't know what else to say. She closed her eyes and tightened her fist at the thought of her aunt and her husband.

After attempting to calm herself for several more minutes, Hannah leaned back in her chair and sat for a few minutes, wondering what new lesson God was getting ready to walk her through.

No, Lord. I refuse to deal with this right now. It's too hard, Hannah said, standing.

Nothing is too hard for me. You should know that by now, God continued.

Hannah had lived with her aunt Loretta for a short time when her mom was struggling with making good choices during Hannah's pre-teen and teen years. During that time, her aunt's husband would touch her inappropriately and tell her she would go into foster care if she told anyone. It got so bad she had to tell her best friend back then, and her friend finally pushed her to tell her dad after he had reached out to her aunt inquiring about Hannah and wanting to see her. Hannah shuddered at the thought as she reflected.

Stroking her arms, she shook her head as if she could shake the memories from her mind.

After finally finding the courage to tell her dad everything, he encouraged her to report it to her school counselor, and she did. The counselor also contacted the Division of Family and Children Services to file a report, which resulted in Hannah's dad receiving full custody of her. The only good part about it all was going to live with her dad. Her aunt then began to harass her and told her she was a liar. Hannah shook her head as she remembered how ugly her aunt Loretta was to her. She was only a child. Hannah hadn't thought about it in years. She had vowed to put it all behind her, and she wasn't about to deal with it now.

She refused to have her aunt or her husband anywhere near her or her baby girl. As her heart pounded, she spoke to the storm that was trying to creep in and wreck her peaceful existence, and she didn't understand. Hadn't she been obedient to God.

The faith steps she had to take to open the center were minor compared to facing her Aunt Loretta and Satan himself.

"Peace, you will be still by any means necessary."

CHAPTER SEVEN

Monday, November 11

After finally receiving the emails about more grant approvals on Friday, Hannah couldn't hold back her excitement. She pumped her fist in the air as she got dressed.

"Praise the Lord. Thank You, Jesus," she shouted. One grant was for forty thousand dollars. The other was for fifteen thousand. She would have to apply again for them to be renewed the following year, but that was standard. She knew that was another sign from the Lord that He was with her. With these grants, the other two small grants, and the other funding she continued to receive through donations, there was no doubt she could open the center.

Hannah rejoiced once again as she undid her pin curls for her go-to twist out style. If she was frugal, what she had could carry them through the first year. Even though the funding was not enough for her to receive a salary, her faith had increased a little more, regardless of the madness from her aunt showing up and now living with her mom.

With a scheduled follow-up appointment today for her arm, Hannah had taken off another personal day from work. She had also scheduled an appointment to check out another building as she had been doing since putting in her resignation. She and Levi had visited them by faith, and she was more encouraged each time. Today, her mom and Ms. Priscilla had promised to go with her. Her mom was off on Mondays, and Ms. Priscilla's salon was also closed.

The building she was going to check out was closer to the shelter and in a strip mall in a high-traffic area. This would be the fourth building she'd gone to inquire about, and she actually had the money to put down on it.

The first one was too far out. The second one was too expensive. The last one was too old, and the landlord wanted them to fix the issues, which were many. Hannah prayed this would be the one. It was in the perfect location, and the monthly rent was more reasonable than the others. She decided she would trust God with the details and with providing more manna in the coming months and days.

Hannah also didn't have enough to hire anyone, so she would have to rely upon April and Tamela for now, and her mom had told her that her aunt could help as a crisis counselor with her background in mental health. Hannah had looked at her mom like she had lost her mind. No, her aunt couldn't be anywhere around her. She couldn't have her assisting her. She understood her aunt was willing to volunteer to lighten her load, but Hannah didn't understand why her mom would think she could just move past what she'd experienced with her aunt and her aunt's husband. Yes, she understood God's instructions about forgiveness, but she wasn't ready.

Lord, make provisions for a crisis counselor. Send the help from somewhere else. Maybe I can do it for now, at least until I have the funding to hire someone.

After dropping Ariel off at daycare, Hannah headed over to her doctor's appointment. She was one of the first patients, so she was in and out. She had received more positive news. Her sprain was almost healed, but she was still instructed to keep on the sling for another week. Next, she made her way to her mom's apartment to pick her up to head to the building appointment. Pulling into The Cove Apartment Homes, as she drove through the gates, she prayed her aunt wasn't there. She didn't want her spoiling her good mood. After passing the first four buildings, Hannah quickly pulled in a parking space in front of Building 5 and headed to her mom's door. She needed to hurry because she had to pick up Ms. Priscilla next and make her appointment on time, and she hoped they could still grab a bite to eat and do a little shopping before it was time for her to pick up Ariel from daycare. Grateful her mom lived on the first floor, Hannah knocked on the door, and heard her aunt's voice. The anger Hannah had been feeling on and off was back again.

She closed her eyes. *Lord, I don't want to deal with her. She didn't believe me when I told her about that man touching me back then. She even harassed me about reporting it, and she stayed with him. Am I supposed to feel sorry for her situation? Why is she showing up now? I haven't seen nor spoken to her in years. What about me and my feelings?* Hannah prayed in her heart as she stood there for a few more seconds, considering returning to her car and calling her mom later. It was too late. Her mom opened the door.

Hannah stepped back, staring past her mom, locking eyes with her aunt who sat on the couch. Aunt Loretta averted her eyes, trying to look like she was engrossed with what was on the T.V. screen. Hannah then turned her eyes to look at her mom.

"Hey, sweetheart," her mom said, leaning in to give her a hug. "Come on in."

Hannah hesitated before stepping inside. "Hey, Mama. You ready?"

"Hannah, how are you?" her aunt Loretta finally asked in a low tone.

"I'm good," Hannah said, with her back turned facing her mother. "You ready?" she asked again, trying to avoid any conversation with her aunt.

"I'm not going to be able to go with you this morning. Loretta has been having some issues with Malcolm. She filed for a divorce, and he has been harassing and threatening to harm her."

"O...kay. It took her this long to see Satan for who he is," Hannah said, shifting her weight.

"Is Ms. Priscilla still able to go?" her mom asked, ignoring her comment.

"Yes, but I was hoping you could too, and I was looking forward to us grabbing lunch and doing a little shopping or just hanging and looking around a few stores," Hannah replied, still avoiding eye contact with her aunt.

"I'm sorry. I was looking forward to it, but as I said, Malcolm's had been giv—"

"What does that have to do with you?" Hannah snapped.

"She's my sister. I have to be here for her too."

"Mama, no disrespect, but I could care less about that evil being of a husband of hers, and Auntie should have left him long before now," Hannah said, regretting how her words came out to her mom, but she was disappointed and annoyed now.

"Sweetie?"

"No, she's right. I should have recognized it a long time ago..." Aunt Loretta said.

"Anyway, Mama, I've gotta go so I can pick up Ms. Priscilla," Hannah said, cutting her aunt off. She had to get out of there before she said something else she regretted to her.

"Do you have a few minutes to talk?" her mom asked.

"No. I love you, Mama. I'll call you later and tell you how it went. Maybe we can hang out another time," Hannah said, darting out the door, almost tripping over the doormat.

"Oh, okay. Love you too," her mom stated.

Hannah's heart broke at the sadness in her mom's voice, but she was still not ready to deal with anything connected with her aunt and her disgusting husband.

Lord, are you sure about this? She practically jogged to return to the security of her car. Fighting back tears, Hannah started the engine and headed over to pick up Ms. Priscilla. *I don't want to deal with this. It's all in my past. My past is behind me. I only wanted to spend some time with my mom. Why did Aunt Loretta have to be here?*

Forgive. Give her grace.

Lord, why do I have to even talk to her at all?

You must forgive and give grace as I have graced you in order to minister effectively.

After those words, Hannah connected her phone's Bluetooth and clicked her phone to play the Christian Apologetics podcast she'd found interesting a few days ago—anything to not think about her past and having to deal with her aunt or her aunt's husband.

When she arrived at Ms. Priscilla's house, her mentor was waiting on the porch for her. She stood and walked to the passenger side and climbed in. Hannah attempted to respond with excitement in her voice, but Ms. Priscilla eyed her as if she could see straight through to her soul.

"Mama couldn't make it?" Ms. Priscilla asked.

"No. She had to stay with my aunt."

"Is everything okay?"

"No. Something about my aunt having issues with her husband now that she's filed for divorce."

"Oh my."

"I don't know why anyone is surprised with his actions. I've known he's been evil for years. That's why I haven't had anything to do with

Aunt Loretta since I was a teenager. She chose him instead of believing me."

Hannah could feel Ms. Priscilla's eyes on her. She was silent for a moment before she spoke. "Sweetness, you have to release that unforgiveness."

"Ms. Priscilla, I can't help it. I'm angry. I thought I could face this. I thought I had forgiven them, but this is even harder than the steps it took to forgive Mama."

"It's only difficult because you are having trouble releasing it to Christ. Do you believe He can heal you in that area of your life? Do you believe He can give you the strength to forgive them for real?"

Hannah sat quietly for a few moments. Ms. Priscilla's words shook her once again. She could still feel her mentor's eyes on her. *Why can't I get some time off? This is too much.*

Ms. Priscilla spoke again. "Do you believe he can heal that area of your life, Hannah?"

"I honestly don't know," Hannah finally said. "It's too painful to think about. I thought I had given it all to him, but I guess I haven't."

"But you must. That's the only way, sweetheart. You have to hand it over to him so you can move in ministry without hindrance."

"Can you pray for me to find the strength to give it to him?"

"Of course. Once we get to your appointment, I will. How far away are we?"

"About five minutes."

Hannah was scheduled to meet with the leasing agent at 9:30. Her hands trembled as she neared the destination. She gripped the steering wheel tighter, trying to calm herself. It wasn't just the meeting for the building. It was also needing to trust God with the forgiveness and for the favor of all that was happening.

So That You May Live

A few minutes early, Hannah and Ms. Priscilla pulled into a parking space away from the building.

"Is that it?" Ms. Priscilla asked, pointing across from where they were parked. The building was next to what appeared to be a pet store.

"Yes. I believe so."

"Are we able to pray right now?" Ms. Priscilla asked.

"That would be great," Hannah said.

"Let's join hands."

Hannah followed her instructions, turning to face her mentor.

Ms. Priscilla began, "Dear heavenly father, I come to You on behalf of your daughter, Hannah.

She is struggling with releasing more pain from past abuse. We know You know all about it. Give her the strength to release her aunt Loretta and Loretta's husband, forgiving them. Help her to understand that Christ died for them as well, and You desire them to be saved and delivered as You saved and delivered Hannah. Give Hannah a heart of flesh in this situation so that You can penetrate it, softening it. May she release and forgive, so it doesn't hinder where You are taking her. Also, please lead her in the right direction needed to locate the building You have for the women's development center. Give her favor with the owners of this building, if this is the one. Provide the resources and individuals needed to bring this vision to pass. We thank You in advance for the mighty works we know You will do through Hannah and the others who will serve Your women. Cause her and the women to walk in wholeness. Your will be done. We give You glory and praise, in Jesus' name. Amen."

"Amen," Hannah said, crying. "Lord, help me. I can't do this on my own."

Embracing Hannah, Ms. Priscilla replied, "He is your help. Sweetheart, God's got you. You've got to know that."

"Thanks for praying for me. And I'm a little nervous."

"Honey, all the great men and women who God used in scripture have had their fears. You've read about Moses."

"Oh, yeah. He was fearful, but God did use him in a great way," Hannah said.

"He absolutely did, and He will also use you," Ms. Priscilla said, patting Hannah on the shoulder.

"Now, let's get in here and receive the favor of God."

"Let's do it," Hannah said.

As they climbed out of her car, Hannah felt a tinge of courage, and the worries about her aunt's presence had floated from her mind. She started walking toward the building, and Ms. Priscilla walked behind her. It was as if her mentor had strategically thought of that, so she would catch her if she attempted to turn back or run. *I'm not sure if I'm ready for this.*

"You've got this," Ms. Priscilla whispered with her hand on Hannah's shoulder as if she could read her mind.

Hannah smiled to herself as they neared the door. It opened, and a brown-skinned, middle-aged African-American woman stepped out. Her silky black hair hung around her shoulders. She was dressed in a navy blue skirt, white blouse, and matching navy jacket. Her smile was contagious. Hannah greeted the woman, shaking her hand, then Ms. Priscilla greeted her. As the woman stepped aside to let them in, Hannah took a deep breath and felt a sudden peace. God's presence was with her, and He knew all the details. If this wasn't the one, she would keep looking until she found it.

Thank You for choosing me, Lord Jesus. Give me the words to speak. Remove all fear.

CHAPTER EIGHT

· · · • • • • ● • • • • · · ·

Two Months Later

Wednesday, January 12

It is better to obey later than to never have obeyed at all. Okay, maybe not. That's still disobedience, right? Well, God, thank You for Your grace in my failure to follow Your instructions before now. Thank You for entrusting me and not choosing someone else because You could've, Hannah thought as she stood at the entrance of the So That You May Live Women's Development Center, her heart leaping with anticipation.

After searching for weeks for the right affordable building, she was blessed with one only a few blocks from the House of Hope Women's Shelter right next to the pet store. It was the last building she had checked out with Ms. Priscilla. She wished her mom had been there with her instead of having to stay with her aunt, but she understood. Hannah felt a mix of fear and joy as she signed the paperwork and took possession of the keys a week later. It was the most remarkable feeling. Hannah's mentor was right. God had given her favor here. Things seemed to move rather quickly after signing the paperwork to lease the building. She had come over today to make sure everything was ready for the grand opening on Saturday.

The sun's gentle rays shone through the large glass window at the front of the building, next to the matching glass door. The rays cast a warm glow on the newly lavender-painted walls. The scent of fresh paint seemed to mix with the fragrance of hope. Hannah took a deep breath, her hand grazing the worn surface of the donated reception desk. Although she didn't have enough funding to hire a receptionist just yet, she was more encouraged now. All she needed would come. She had trusted God, and here she stood. A sense of purpose flowed through her veins, as she knew this was where she was meant to be. The journey had not been easy—from securing enough funds to the favor she received so quickly to open and operate in their county.

The board members and her family had all worked alongside her to pull it all together. Her dad and Aunt Melissa had even traveled an hour to assist. His brother, her uncle Joseph, hadn't been feeling well, so he couldn't make it out. Hannah prayed for God to keep her uncle's health. He and his wife, Aunt Melissa, had helped her dad raise her while she and her dad lived with them. They had both taught her so much, and they meant the world to her.

Her friend, Tamela, had been a tremendous help too. She had assisted with painting and setting up the center. She wished her other friend, Robin, was there to experience this with her, but she would give her a call when she got a chance. She had missed Robin's call a few days ago.

After sharing the good news of opening the center with her pastor at Giver of Life Ministries a few weeks ago, some of her church members had even agreed to help by donating more funds and equipment. Hannah was ecstatic at their generosity. This was even more of a confirmation that God was in it. *His favor for sure,* she thought.

With the center being blocks from House of Hope, the women could walk there if needed because many of them didn't have their own transportation.

Beaming with pride, she walked through the center, taking in the rooms filled with possibilities.

Hannah turned up the thermostat to seventy-eight to ward off the winter chill in the air. It wasn't a very large space, but there was enough to complete the mission.

As we grow, maybe the Lord will expand us. Yes, if we are here to make an impact, let's impact, Hannah thought, pumping her fist in the air, feeling more confident than before. She couldn't hold back her excitement now. Her faith had grown a little more through this process, and she was sure it would grow even more. *Wow. God did it. I couldn't have ever done this on my own.*

Actually, the reality of it was a bit terrifying. Nope, there was no turning back.

There was the counseling room where women could share their stories, find solace, and receive guidance on their path to healing. There was also a small donations storage space, which she had named Hannah's Closet. It would serve as extra resources for the women in need. In the main meeting area, there was a space set aside for education, skills training, and workshops. Lining the back wall were the eight donated computers she had received.

Hannah could already see the center bustling with life—women laughing, learning, building relationships, and supporting one another. She imagined the walls echoing with stories of resilience, triumph, and transformation. The So That You May Live Women's Development Center would work in conjunction with the local shelters and churches and be a place where women could rebuild their lives and discover their strengths. She had so many more event ideas she was eager to run by the board.

Hannah knew the road ahead wouldn't be without its challenges. She would need to navigate through and learn even more about fundraising, engaging the community, and ensuring the center's sustainability with even more funding. Yes, the board would continue to assist with the process, but she was the visionary. Therefore, she had to oversee it all. Doubts and uncertainties would arise, but she didn't want to give up.

Hannah walked into her office next. It was a closet-sized space adorned with inspirational quotes and pictures of her with family and friends. She sighed, taking a seat at her desk she'd found at a yard sale. She sat in her old office chair from home. It had been sitting in the garage, only used when Levi hung out in there, enjoying the breeze, which wasn't until the fall. She patted the worn arms and relaxed, grateful it was comfortable because she knew she would spend a lot of time in it. She then smiled at the picture of her husband and daughter in the lavender wooden frame on her desk, grateful for such a beautiful family.

Hannah then bowed her head, and prayed, *Dear Lord, I want to say thank You for entrusting me with this development center. I know there is so much more I will learn as we launch and begin to serve the community. I know that You will continue to be with me and walk beside me. Even as obstacles arise, give me wisdom to overcome them and not want to run away from them. You have done so much in such a short amount of time, and I thank You in advance for what will take place in this space. The women who enter these doors are counting on me and whoever You send to assist with the vision, and I pray we will not let them down, in Jesus' name. Amen.*

Hannah lifted her head and said, "The So That You May Live Women's Development Center is the only women's development center in the Forest Park area. That's a lot of pressure, Lord."

At those words, she stood and headed out. Everything was perfect for the grand opening.

CHAPTER NINE

Saturday, January 15

"Thanks to all of our efforts in advance, we can now better help the women in our community to thrive and embrace a life of empowerment," Hannah exclaimed, her voice carrying over the crowd as she waved the large pair of red scissors she'd used to cut the ceremonial ribbon for the official grand opening of her new women's center.

She took in the cheers from the small group of supporters who stood before her. Hannah glanced at the smiling faces of the board members, her family, church members, volunteers, and her friends April and Tamela. She was grateful they had stood with her the whole way. Her eyes were brimming with tears of joy as she stood still so her husband could snap a few photos, then she spun around and wrapped her arms around her mother who was beaming with pride.

"I'm so proud of you, Hannah," her mom stated, looking her in the eyes and giving her a big hug.

Hannah wiped away the lone tear that trickled down her cheek. "Thank you so much, Mama. You don't know how much I appreciate those words coming from you and you being here by my side. The two of us have overcome so much, and I'm grateful that you are standing here with me today. I love you." Hannah wiped away more tears.

"You know I wouldn't miss this. I just hate I couldn't help with the preparations because of my hours at the post office and trying to help your aunt out with her situation."

"Mama, I'm just glad you're here now," Hannah said, hugging her mom again, trying to remain calm at the mention of her aunt's drama with that man.

"Oh, stop all that," Levis said, laughing and wrapping his arms around her waist from behind. Hannah slapped his hand. He then stepped around her to hug and kiss her mom on the cheek.

"You are such a clown," Hannah said.

"You love this clown though," Levi said, whirling around to give her a kiss.

"I do. Thank you for always supporting me," Hannah said, wrapping her hands around his neck, pulling him into a longer, lingering kiss. He lifted her off her feet into a bear hug.

"Alright, alright," her dad teased as they pulled away from each other's embrace.

Hannah nearly leaped up and down as she turned toward her dad, Aunt Melissa, Uncle Joseph, and her mother-in-law, Mama Jefferson. She smiled at her day-one supporters and reached for Ariel.

"Hey, Mama's sweet girl," Hannah sang, lifting Ariel up from beside her dad and showering her with kisses.

Ariel giggled and said, "Mommy, I'm too big to be picked up."

"Well, excuse me, ma'am," Hannah said, putting her daughter down. Ariel attempted to fix her lavender and black tutu, which Hannah had made to go with her So That You May Live t-shirt. She had added a pair of thick black leggings beneath it because of the winter air. Her daughter looked adorable, minus Ariel's large coat, which covered the full view of the outfit.

"I'm a big girl," Ariel said, looking down at her clothes, struggling to straighten out her tutu.

"Yes, you are," Hannah said, assisting her daughter and giving her another kiss on the cheek.

"Are we going in your new place now?" Ariel asked, looking up, smiling, and grabbing Hannah's dad's hand. Her bright eyes danced in the unusual sunlight of the moderately cold January day.

Yes. Let's get ready to get inside. I love you, princess," Hannah said before heading to let the guests know what was next.

"I love you too, Mama," Ariel said.

She is such a joy, Hannah thought, as she noticed others in the crowd smiling at her and Ariel's interaction.

Thinking about her new responsibilities, Hannah was still nervous because her daughter was still so young. Her mother-in-law said she would help with picking Ariel up from daycare and allowing her to spend a few days a week with her because Levi worked late, and Hannah would need to stay late sometimes at the center as well. That would at least reduce their monthly daycare bill, but she still would miss time with her daughter. That would be an adjustment for her.

As she attempted to get everyone's attention, Hannah's heart swelled with joy as she looked at her family once again. She knew they would be here. They had never let her down. The only ones missing were her five-year-old niece, Neveah, and her sister, Brittany, because Brittany had to work and Neveah was with her dad's parents.

Everyone seemed to be deep in conversation and their voices had elevated. Hannah spoke as loud as she could, but only a few heard her.

"Alright. Let's get this party started," Levi yelled, stepping over next to Hannah after noticing she was struggling to get the crowd's attention.

"Yes, I can't wait for you all to see the inside and grab some of the refreshments we have for you," Hannah said a little louder this time. She then reached into her black blazer pocket for the keys to the center. Then she heard a familiar voice of congratulations.

It was Aunt Loretta.

Why is she here? Hannah thought, frozen in place. Her anger returned at the thought of her aunt being at her grand opening. Yes, she had been cordial with her lately after her mom explained how important they both were to her, but she hadn't invited her aunt to celebrate with them. She slowly turned, trying to paste on a smile. She then turned and eyed her mom who gave her a half smile.

"She wanted to come and congratulate you in person," her mom whispered.

"Thank you," she finally said, unable to look into her aunt's eyes.

Hannah squeezed her fists together, releasing them when she felt the key stabbing her palm. She took a deep breath. Aunt Loretta walked toward her and wrapped her arms around her. Hannah stiffened, not returning the gesture, then she realized the guests' eyes were on her, and they were waiting to go inside. Not wanting to make a scene, she side-hugged her aunt quickly and backed away.

"Thank you for coming," Hannah whispered, trying to mask her anger.

She fumbled with the keys but finally opened the door and stood for a moment, taking it all in.

"It looks amazing," her mom stated, stepping beside Hannah.

"Yes, it does. It turned out beautiful, Mama."

"You will do great work for this community."

"Thanks again, Mama," Hannah said, doing her best to hide her disappointment in her mom. *Why didn't she ask me before inviting Aunt Loretta?*

"And, by the way, I love my shirt," her mom said, spinning around, modeling the lavender and black glittered So That You May Live T-shirt Hannah had had made by a woman she'd met at one of her business networking meetups.

"Yes. Aren't they fabulous, hunty!" Hannah said, opening her blazer to reveal her t-shirt and twirling around. She then turned to wave the rest of the guests inside, hoping her aunt had left. No such luck. She was standing beside a woman Hannah didn't recognize. *Lord, help me to stay calm.* Determined to not let her aunt's presence ruin one of the best moments of her life, Hannah took another deep breath and smiled again, waving the crowd inside. "Alright everyone, come on in."

Bursting with excitement, she stepped aside, her arms outstretched, welcoming the women and other guests into the So That You May Live Women's Development Center. Also wearing the organization's t-shirt, her friends and volunteers, April and Tamela, entered to assist with passing out refreshments. Hannah's pastor, Pastor Richardson, had come earlier to bless the building and to pray with Hannah. Afterward, he reminded her that prayer needed to remain essential as she moved forward on this new journey. Ms. Priscilla had several clients today, so she said she would stop by on her break for a few minutes.

As the crowd entered, the smell of freshly brewed coffee began to fill the air, and the sunlight seemed to invite them in as it shone bright through the large front window, illuminating the space. As the guests looked around, there were murmurs of amazement as they all took in the lavender walls filled with a generous amount of images of women who had made an impact around the world, as well as inspirational quotes. The smell of fresh flowers also tickled Hannah's nostrils as she directed people to sit at the circular tables in the center of the main meeting space. She made a mental note to thank April for the beautiful lavender centerpieces.

It doesn't even look like an older building now, she thought, smiling.

After getting everyone settled, Hannah stood before the small crowd and officially welcomed them.

She shared the center's vision and mission and described the other areas in the facility. She explained the different programs and workshops they would begin hosting. Finally, she shared how excited she was to help women walk in their God-given purpose, to offer them group counseling services using a certified counselor, who had finally signed up to volunteer and to assist them with learning different skills, training, and preparation for seeking employment.

As Hannah neared the end of her introductions, her mom and mother-in-law were assisting with serving more coffee and refreshments. Her dad, Aunt Melissa, and Uncle Joseph beamed with pride as they listened and took it all in. She felt their support and prayers. She then smiled at Levi as he blew her a kiss and mouthed, "I'm proud of you" from the back of the room.

Hannah mingled with the guests as they finished their refreshments, avoiding her Aunt Loretta like an illness trying to overtake her body. Ms. Priscilla came in a few moments later. Hannah greeted her with a tight squeeze.

"Ms. Priscilla, you made it! I can't believe this is all happening."

"Why not? I told you God would do it. He was waiting on you, sweetness," her mentor said, smiling.

"Thank you for pushing and praying me through."

"To God be all the glory. I am serving Him by serving as your mentor."

"I'm grateful," said Hannah.

"This place is beautiful. I'm so proud of you."

"Thanks. It did turn out really nice. Would you like some refreshments?"

"I will take some."

After Hannah let her mom know that Ms. Priscilla needed some refreshments, she left her mentor in the care of her dad, Uncle Joseph, and Aunt Melissa as she continued to move around the room to greet her guests. She met a few women from other cities in Georgia who wanted to collaborate with her in building up and empowering women. Hannah couldn't believe what she was hearing.

Am I dreaming?

As the guests continued to mingle, Hannah and Tamela gave a few groups at a time a tour of the facility while the others enjoyed getting to know one another.

After returning to the meeting space of the center, Hannah held a question-and-answer session.

"Will you be hosting Bible study here as you've been doing on Zoom with us?" Simone asked, one of the younger women from House of Hope Women's Shelter.

"Absolutely. You know that's my jam. The Word is our foundation."

"Sounds great. I'm looking forward to it. I am so excited for you," the young woman squealed.

"Thank you so much," Hannah replied, stepping over to give Simone a hug.

"Any more questions?" Hannah asked, moving back to the front.

"Yes, I have a question," a woman she didn't recognize shouted above the chatter among the tables.

"Go ahead," Hannah said.

"Will you have other services like clothing and toy drives around the holidays?"

"Yes. I'm glad you asked that question. I've been talking with the board about kicking off a clothing drive in March. I would love to use the small room down the hall here," Hannah said, pointing, "to continue donations throughout the year. I've named it Hannah's Closet."

"Ohhh, I love it," one of the guests sang.

"Thanks so much. I can't explain how much joy obeying God and finally opening has brought me. Thank you all for the much-appreciated support," Hannah said.

After the other guests and volunteers, her dad, uncle, and Aunt Melissa had left, Hannah's mother, husband, and aunt stayed behind to help clean up.

Once Hannah finished vacuuming the floor, her aunt walked over, attempting to strike up a conversation. "I'm so happy for you. This is going to be great."

"Thanks," Hannah said between clenched teeth.

"You look amazing, and you have such a beautiful family."

Unable to hold her frustration with her aunt's presence any longer, Hannah blurted out, "Aunt Loretta, why are you here? You haven't reached out to me since I was a child."

"I know, and I'm sorry. I always ask your mom about you."

"Please keep your apology," Hannah spat.

"I am truly sorry, Hannah. Malc—"

"Don't you dare say that evil man's name in my presence."

"Babe, don't do this to yourself. That man is behind you," Levi said.

"Well, I thought he was. Then, she shows up out of the blue," Hannah said.

"Hannah, we are going through a divorce. It took me a long time to leave him, but I finally did."

"Why? Because he molested someone else's daughter? Is that it, Aunt Loretta?"

"Hannah, I'm sorry," Aunt Loretta said, tears welling in her eyes.

"I told you to keep your apology, now get out," Hannah said, not moved by her aunt's words.

"Sweetheart, I'm sorry. I invited Loretta. I thought it would be okay," her mom said.

"Why would you think it would be okay for her to be here, Mama?" Hannah screamed.

"You know I love you, and this silence between you two has gone on long enough. I know that God wants us all to make amends, just like He did for me and you," Hannah's mom continued.

"Well, it won't happen tonight, that's for sure," Hannah said, walking away.

"Let's just finish and get out of here so we can pick up Ariel from my mom's," Levi said as he followed Hannah toward her office. "Babe, are you okay?"

"No," Hannah said, her back to the door.

"Don't do this to yourself. You have come so far from where you were just a few years ago."

"I can't do this, Levi," Hannah said, turning to face her husband. "I know God desires for me to forgive Aunt Loretta as I forgave Mama, but she hasn't said a word to me in all these years. Now, she conveniently shows up when she's had enough of his treatment towards her. Where was she when I cried all those tears as a teenage girl, wondering why she seemed to abandon me? I thought I was over this, but I guess I'm not. We used to hang out together when I lived with her. She was there when Mama wasn't back then...until I told what her husband did to me. I've dealt with enough pain," she explained, her voice trailing off as she wiped away the flood of tears blinding her.

Hannah turned to take a seat at her desk. Levi came around the other side, pulled her from her chair, and she buried her head in his chest, her chest heaving. Levi remained silent, only rubbing her back. He finally spoke softly.

"I love you."

"I love you too."

"You are one of the strongest women I know. We are going to pray together for you to trust God with this in the same way you trusted Him with opening this center, the miscarriages, and the endometriosis treatments—even with you and your mom's relationship. God wants to heal and restore this as well, babe."

"I believe He can, but what if I don't want Him to. Is that a bad thing? How can I trust her?" Hannah said, looking into her husband's eyes.

"It's called grief, and you've buried it for years of your life, so it's easier not dealing with it. But you know the Word now."

"I know...I know...forgive others of their trespasses so God can forgive us of ours," Hannah said, lifting her head and waving her arms as if trying to erase the scriptures she'd just recited.

"That's His Word, and you have to do this, babe. Don't think this is just a coincidence that this came across your path now, after all these years. The Lord wants to use you in the lives of these women."

"Levi, this is one of the hardest steps I've had to take. How can I forgive someone who harmed me as a child, and my aunt—my blood relative—blamed me because it was her raggedy husband."

"Well, tell me how you really feel about him."

Hannah cracked a smile. "Stop being a clown, man. I don't want to laugh."

"I want you to crush this obstacle as you did the others. I don't want to see you shed anymore tears.

It's time to soar in Christ."

"I want the same, but what if I can't?"

"You can't in your strength, but you can in the strength of Christ," Levi said.

"Can I ask you a question?" Hannah asked, still looking at her husband.

"What is it?"

"Why aren't you angry with her? Why don't you hate him?"

"Because God won't allow me to. I have to be strong for you and Ariel. Plus, he can't hurt you any longer, and your aunt is finally realizing her wrong in it all. I got you," Levi said, pulling Hannah back toward him.

"I thank God for you so much," Hannah said, the tears flowing again. This time Levi wiped them away.

"You've got this, and I've got you. One step at a time. Allow Christ to do it again. You are more than a conqueror."

After those words, Hannah knew she needed prayer and strength. Levi seemed to know what to do without her speaking. She bowed her head as he began to pray for Christ to intervene. She knew he had to if she was going to be effective and successful in this ministry. *God, I didn't sign up for this*, she thought as her husband prayed.

CHAPTER TEN

Tuesday, January 18

Since Hannah's first official scheduled group of women weren't due to arrive until next week, and she had been working long hours to get the center up and running, she decided to take an hour lunch break and treat herself to Zaxby's. She needed to take a breath, and she would take it wherever she could get it.

Placing her computer in her black laptop bag, grabbing her purse, and throwing her cell phone inside, Hannah stepped outside, locked up, and walked a few doors down to the Zaxby's on the corner of the strip mall. She promised herself that she would only check her personal email and watch some Youtube videos to pass the time. When she got inside, she hopped in the line behind an older gentleman who was flirting with the woman in front of him. Hannah laughed as the woman waved him away. She'd just missed the lunch rush. Hannah loved this place. Their seasoned fries were the best. She knew this wasn't the healthiest place to eat, but she needed some comfort food at the moment, and the exchange between the two in front of her made her day.

After ordering her food, she grabbed a booth at the back of the restaurant and logged onto her laptop using the restaurant's Wi-Fi network and opened her personal email. There was something from her former principal. Hannah frowned. *What does she want?* She began reading the message and stared at the screen for several moments.

How can this woman be telling me she's filing an abandonment of contract claim with the state, and I have to pay up to $2,500 for breaking my contract when she told me to put my resignation in writing? I even checked with the district office about it.

Hannah wanted to leave and never look back the same day that child hit her with that stool, but she remained until the second week in December, before Christmas break. She wanted to scream and cry at the same time. *This is not happening. I want to keep my license in good standing, and I don't have that kind of money to pay out right now. I just opened the center.*

Unable to finish the remainder of the email, Hannah closed it and shut down her computer. She fought back tears as she waited for her number to be called. She couldn't call her husband because he was probably out in the field monitoring his crew of utility workers. Her mom was at work and couldn't pick up.

Ms. Priscilla had clients, and her dad was at work as well, so the Holy Spirit led her to call her Aunt Melissa, Uncle Joseph's wife. She was always encouraging, and Hannah needed it.

Just then, her number was called, so she headed to the counter to retrieve her food. Her appetite was pretty much gone, but she sat back down and ate as much as she could. Hannah then asked for a container and placed the leftovers inside and called her aunt who picked up on the second ring.

"Well, hey niece. How are you? What's going on with you?"

"I'm feeling a little stressed at the moment."

"Why? What's up?"

"I just got an email from my hateful former principal stating that she is reporting that I abandoned my contract."

"What?" her aunt yelled through the phone.

"Yes, Auntie. That woman was no support to me or the other teachers. She never really did much to the student who hit me with that stool. He was still doing the same things before I left."

"That's awful. You did put in your resignation, right?"

"Yes. That's what she told me to do. I did it back in November, and I stayed through December, until we went on break. Some of the other teachers left with no notice at all. How is she going to come after me?"

"I don't know, but don't you worry. Things will work out."

"I don't want to lose my teaching license, and I don't have $2,500 to pay the district for breaking my contract, Auntie."

"We have always taught you to trust God, no matter what. She can't take what God has given, and God called you out, so just trust Him to fix this."

"I don't know, Auntie. This is a lot of stress. Maybe I should go back into the classroom. I haven't really started meeting with the ladies yet."

"Don't you dare do that to yourself. And just how are you going to make that happen? You already have signed the lease on that building, and how can you just leave those women stranded with no services?"

"God can get somebody else to do it. I didn't know it would be so hard."

"You listen to me: Trust in God. Has He ever failed you?"

"No...but."

"No buts, missy. He has never failed you, and He won't now."

"You're right."

"I know I am. Watch Him work out this thing with your teaching license."

"Maybe I can write her back and mention her lack of support and the assault by the student."

"You should definitely do that. Stand up for yourself. Don't let anyone bully you."

"Thanks, Auntie. I have a great circle of support. You all keep me lifted."

"That's what we're here for."

"Alright. I will respond to her email right now before I head back to the center."

"Where are you now?"

"I'm at Zaxby's."

"Oh, Lord. You love that place. When you get to my age, you will have to watch that salt intake."

"Really, Auntie? But it's so good."

"Lord, you sound like your uncle. You will see one day. That's why he's been back and forth at the doctor."

"How is he doing?"

"He's doing a little better. He's hardheaded. He has to eat healthier, and he doesn't want to."

"Tell him to do it for me," Hannah said.

"I will."

"I love you, Auntie. I always feel better after talking to you."

"I'll talk to you soon. Don't wait so long to call."

"I won't."

After speaking to Aunt Melissa, Hannah reopened her laptop and responded to her former principal's email. She told her truth, standing up for her and the other teachers who might still be teaching at the school.

Hannah began the email by informing her if she continued trying to go after her teaching license she would send her email over to an attorney with her true reason for leaving and file a lawsuit against her and the district. She didn't really want to have to do anything like that, but she needed to protect her professional credentials.

Mrs. Garrett, instead of attempting to bully your teachers, you should put that energy into supporting them more, Hannah wrote. *As you know, most teachers don't teach for the money. They teach because they love the students and want to make an impact in their lives. May I ask you why you chose the field? Great leaders are those who serve and support. You didn't do much of that for us at Rocklake. For example, you never really supported me in the incident with Jamal. You pretty much blamed me for not using specific strategies with the student as if I could control that child's explosive anger. I did what was expected of me. I asked to have the behavior specialist get involved. You made me feel as if I was bothering you when I asked about it. The student threw a stool and hit me. I could have been seriously injured, but you didn't seem to care. I loved teaching, but then I came to the conclusion that I couldn't win in such a hostile environment with no support.*

After Hannah sent her reply, she felt another sense of peace in her spirit as she did the day she put in her resignation. She closed her computer and packed up, grabbing her food as she headed back to the center. Her nerves were more at ease now, and she knew she needed to put all her efforts into the center. She at least needed to try. She couldn't quit that easy. *Lord, please work out this situation with my certification. I won't let this stop me from moving forward.*

CHAPTER ELEVEN

Tuesday, February 13

"Thank you for calling The So That You May Live Women's Development Center. This is Mrs. Jefferson. How may I help you?"

"Hey, sis. This is April. I won't be there to volunteer for the remainder of this week.

Something important came up. I should be back on Monday. So sorry for the inconvenience."

Hannah drew in an exhausted breath. Shaking her head, she pulled the phone away from her ear, hoping April couldn't hear her annoyance. Then, her cell phone pinged with more messages about donations coming in through PayPal. She glanced down, *fifty dollars, $150, and three hundred dollars.* Hannah was grateful for more online donations. They would definitely come in handy. She cleared her phone screen, and after a few seconds, she finally said, "Okay. Thank you for letting me know. I pray everything is okay with you."

"No problem. Thanks for understanding," April said before hanging up.

She made a mental note to transfer the PayPal funds they'd received into her bank account, but at this rate she wouldn't get to it today.

The center had only been opened a month, and this had been happening nonstop with her friend. Tamela was her only other volunteer at the moment. She just knew she would have a ton of help with so many sign-ups at the grand opening, but today was a different story, and one of her friends was letting her down once again. Hannah hadn't heard from half of the individuals who'd signed up, and when she attempted to reach out to them, there was no answer—not even callbacks after she'd left messages. She only had one counselor to volunteer her services, and Ms. Reid couldn't be there as often as Hannah needed, so she found herself hosting *real talk* sessions for the women who weren't able to be a part of Ms. Reid's counseling sessions. She hadn't signed up for this. She knew it wouldn't be easy, but at this point, she wanted to go ahead and wave her white flag and surrender to defeat.

"April could have just called my cell phone or texted me," Hannah whispered to herself.

"Is everything okay?" Tamela asked, walking from the corner where she was straightening the bookshelf.

"Yes. April can't be here for the rest of the week. Are you able to stay a little longer this week if needed?" Hannah asked.

"Yes. I'm able to help out."

"Thanks so much. Just let me know if you can't."

"I don't have anything else going on today. I do work in the evening now part time, but not this evening," Tamela said.

"Yes. You told me."

Tamela hadn't worked since Hannah had known her over three years now. Hannah wondered if Tamela's new job had anything to do with her friend's increase in spending lately. Her husband normally covered all of their household expenses, so she knew it wasn't that. Hannah liked nice things too, but Tamela seemed to show her a new bag or a new pair of heals every week. She thought it was a little excessive, but Hannah chose to mind her own business. She had enough to worry about than to be concerned about her friend's spending habits.

With an hour and a half before Hannah's first session of the day, Tamela assisted her with contacting a few of the local churches to see if they had more volunteers willing to serve at the center. She even called their pastor to see if he knew of anyone else who was willing to help. He couldn't think of anyone. They then tried the local colleges again and were baffled that they still didn't have anyone available for an internship in psychology, counseling, or social work.

Hannah had been at the center from sunup to sundown since the opening, trying to fill in where she lacked in volunteer help and to meet the needs of the women, and it was weighing on her and her husband.

She missed dinner with her family several times a week, and Ariel had spent more time at daycare or with her mother-in-law than she or Levi desired. His work hours didn't bring him home until after 6:30 or 7:00 and so did Hannah's. Feeling weary and tired, she blinked back tears.

"It will get better, sis," Tamela said.

"I pray it does. I can't keep going like this."

"You know I got you as much as I'm able to help."

"I know you do."

She had to admit, the first two weeks were amazing. She was doing something she loved, and she no longer felt the stress of trying to teach a group of young people while worrying if she would have another incident with Jamal or if her class would be overcrowded with kids because teachers were out again.

However, she knew she couldn't continue this way. She would need more consistent help soon for the center's success and for her sanity.

Next, she and Tamela worked on catching up on creating files for women who were interested in the services the center offered. There were several who would benefit from crisis counseling, and Ms. Reid couldn't service all of them. There were more needs than hands to support. Hannah tried to remain focused, but her aunt came to mind again. She and Aunt Loretta had been talking more lately, and her aunt continued to apologize for how she'd treated Hannah in the past. Hannah's heart was softening toward her day by day, but she still wasn't sure if it was a good idea for her to assist at the center.

Lord, why does she seem to be one of my only options? Hannah wondered. She understood her aunt was a retired mental health counselor, and she currently did volunteer work as a crisis counselor, which made her available to assist when needed, but Hannah still wasn't ready to have her so close every day, which is how often she would need her to volunteer. Not to mention, Hannah couldn't understand how her aunt's husband was able to have manipulated her aunt all these years with her training in mental health.

That's crazy, Hannah thought. *How can she really help these women?*

As Tamela worked to organize Hannah's Closet after they'd received more clothing donations, Hannah headed into her office to set up some social media posts before her Integrating Faith Into Daily Life workshop was due to start. As she sat at her desk, she thought back to her reaction to her aunt during the night of the grand opening. God was still dealing with her heart about it. She felt this was all His doing; it was a lesson in trusting Him with her whole heart. Attempting again to focus, Hannah closed her eyes and said a prayer for God to send more hands. Even if she considered bringing her aunt onboard, there was lots of work to do at the center, so she would need more than her. When she couldn't redirect her focus, Hannah stood and checked herself out in the mirror. She had taken more time putting herself together as she took being a full-time entrepreneur seriously. She wanted to look the part at all times, and her husband loved her girl boss look, as he called it. As a teacher, it was mainly about comfort for her. Now, she was enjoying rocking her heels, slacks, and blazers.

After a few minutes of distracting herself more, Hannah took a glance over her shoulder at the digital clock on her desk and returned to her seat. Her time was almost up. She sighed and sat in silence for a few minutes before hearing the women entering the center. She had gone nonstop all day.

She stood, grabbed her worksheets and other materials, and headed into their main meeting space.

After welcoming the women and having them introduce themselves because she noticed some new faces, Hannah said an opening prayer. She began with asking each woman how they would define faith and its importance in their lives. She then shared her personal faith journey with the group and answered some questions they had. Next, she and Tamela passed out the worksheets and assisted the women with identifying areas in their lives where faith could be applied. As they shared, Hannah heard several answers.

"At work."

"In decision making."

"In relationships."

Next, they read about Abraham and discussed the areas where he needed to apply faith.

The women were given a template on how they could apply their faith like Abraham. Simone, one of the younger women from House of Hope Women's Shelter, said, "You always bring it with the Word."

"It's all God, not me, and remember, the Word is our foundation. That's where we begin learning about faith—and through prayer of course."

"I want to apply my faith by growing, so I can come out of that shelter," Simone said.

"Thank you for being vulnerable," said Hannah. "Now, I want you to think about the steps you plan to take to make it happen. Write them on your sheet.

"Got it," said Simone.

"I want to do the same, but it's just not that easy," said Amara, another younger woman from House of Hope Women's Shelter.

"Why do you feel that way?" asked Hannah.

"Because things are so expensive. I never went to college or anything. I did graduate high school. Then, I got married so young to the first guy I met, and he's in prison now for selling drugs. I enjoyed what appeared to be the good life. I didn't want for nothing. I know it wasn't right, but that's how I felt at the time. Now I'm on my own in a shelter."

"You don't have family you can live with?" asked Tamela.

"My family lives out in Tennessee. I can't tell them my situation. I would never hear the end of it. I've never been good enough to them."

"I'm sorry to hear that," said Hannah. "Well, you are more than good enough to God. He has a plan for you," said Hannah. "So, I want you to really think about a plan of action. God will see you through."

"I sure hope so. I want better for myself now," added Amara.

"Then, let's get busy. Write it out and stick to it. I'm here to make sure of that.

"Yes, ma'am," said Simone, seeming excited now.

Hannah loved the way she felt at peace when she was assisting the women. She couldn't believe how so many of various ages and backgrounds lived at House of Hope. She knew that was the purpose of the shelter, to provide shelter for those in need, but she knew God had a greater plan for the women there and for those who didn't live there but wanted to grow and develop in their skills and have any other needs met. This was a joy for her, yet the day-to-day operations were draining her.

***

After another long day, Hannah was glad to have finished a little early. She could hardly keep her eyes open as she made her way to Mama Jefferson's to pick up Ariel. After pulling into the driveway, Hannah lay her head back on the seat for a moment before getting out. Although her daughter had calmed down a bit from her first and second year of life, she was still a ball of energy. Hannah had to muster up enough of her own to spend some time with Ariel.

Mama Jefferson opened the door, and Ariel came bounding into Hannah's arms.

"Mommy!"

"Hey, princess. How was your day?" Hannah asked, squeezing her baby girl.

"It was good. We went over our letters and learned a new one," Ariel sang.

"Oh really? Which one did you learn?" Hannah asked, hugging her mother-in-law and smiling at Ariel.

"We learned the letter *N*. It makes the *nnnnn* sound," Ariel said, demonstrating. "Like the word *nnnooo*."

Hannah and Mama Jefferson burst into laughter.

"You know that word, don't you? You used it all the time when you were a year old," Hannah said.

"Me?" Ariel asked, pointing to herself.

"You sure did and still do sometimes—at least you try," Mama Jefferson added.

"I'm a nice girl, Mommy and Nana. I don't say no to my daycare teacher."

"You better not," Mama Jefferson scolded.

"Alright. Go grab your bag. We have to get home so Mommy can cook."

"Can we have brownies for dinner?"

"Do you mean as a dessert?"

"No, for dinner. No more food. Just brownies."

"Absolutely not, missy. Now go get your bag." Hannah laughed as Ariel dashed down the hall to her room Mama Jefferson had set up for her. She noticed her mother-in-law's look of concern. "Mama, is everything okay?"

"Sweetheart, you have been looking so exhausted lately. Are you getting enough rest?"

"I'm trying, but it is taking a lot of my time at the center. I pray it will get a little easier soon."

"Well, you let those volunteers help you where they can. Don't try to do it all on your own, you hear me?"

"That's one of the problems. I hardly have any volunteers. I only have Tamela and Ms. Reid who are helping out as much as they can right now. April hasn't been there as much," Hannah said as Ariel skipped back into the living room.

"Oh, no. I can help out a little on the days that Ariel is in daycare and when I don't have events at our church."

"Oh, that would be great, Mama. I'm praying I get more help soon."

"How about I come and help out tomorrow for a bit?" Mama Jefferson asked.

"Yes. I could use some extra hands."

"Alright. It's a date," Mama Jefferson said, leaning in to hug Hannah.

"Thanks so much. You don't know how much this means to me."

"You know you don't have to thank me, dear. I'm here for you."

"You ready to go?" Hannah asked Ariel.

"Yesssss."

"Alright. You get on home and try to get to bed a little early. And let that son of mine prepare the dinner."

"He did it the past few nights. I told him I would tonight."

"Alright. Love you all," Mama Jefferson said, leaning down to kiss Ariel on the cheek.

"Love you, Nana," Ariel said.

"I love you too, my darling," Mama Jefferson said, blowing Ariel a kiss.

Ariel beelined her way to the car and began pulling on the door handle, trying to open it.

"Hold on, Ariel. The door is locked."

"Mama, why do the trees lose their leaves again?" Ariel asked out of the blue, as Hannah hit the latch to unlock the doors.

"They lose their leaves because it's still winter right now. They will come back when it gets warmer." Hannah was sure her daughter would be a scientist or something related because she was the most curious little girl she'd ever met.

Once Ariel was secured in her car seat, Hannah climbed onto the driver's seat of her older model Toyota Camry. As she backed out, she took a deep breath and prayed in her heart, *Father, grant me direction and balance. If I'm exhausted right now, I don't want to think about two or three months from now. You have placed this vision in my heart, and You have opened the doors. I need your help.*

CHAPTER TWELVE

Monday, February 27

"Lord, we thank You for this time together. I pray Your will for this center. May the beautiful women before me be empowered by today's workshop and continue to tell others who may need this place and resources You have provided for them. No matter what comes our way, help us to keep moving forward. I give You all the glory for what You will do through each of us, in Jesus' name. Amen," Hannah said.

"Amen," the women said in unison.

Hannah had a little more energy since she had more help from her aunt Loretta, and her mother-in-law continued to assist when she could. Last week, she was able to go home by five, the time the center actually closed. Her aunt had not only helped with crisis counseling over the past two weeks, she'd also assisted Tamela with more of the clerical things Hannah needed to have done. Hannah was glad she'd given her a chance, but she still was uneasy with her there. Yes, she felt a burden had been lifted, and the women loved Aunt Loretta, but Hannah still wasn't sold on the idea of her being there partly because she didn't want to encounter her aunt's husband. She made that clear to her aunt who didn't believe he would try to come around the center. Hannah knew it would take time to overcome their strife from the past and trust her more. Her aunt had even volunteered to come every day to have something to do, but Hannah told her she wasn't needed every day because her mother-in-law was still helping out on Tuesdays and Thursdays.

Hannah passed out affirmation worksheets to the women in attendance. She didn't know why she was a little nervous. She had been running the center for almost two months. Ten eager women sat before her at the used wooden tables in the small meeting area at the front of the center. God had given her the vision for a great workshop that she was trying out for the first time today. She prayed the women would enjoy the presentation, and it would empower them to believe in themselves more. As usual, several of the women present were from House of Hope Women's Shelter. There were also some new faces from Pastor Dickerson's church. He was one of her board members. Two were from her church, Giver of Life Ministries.

After placing handouts and small metal containers, which included pens, sticky notes, and highlighters, on the tables, Hannah was ready. They would begin with affirmations, then they would move into goal setting, interactive discussions, self-care practices, action plans, and more. She was determined to continue making the Word of God their foundation, so she had also created note cards with scriptures on image and self-worth. One of her favorites was Genesis 1:27, how humanity was created in the image of God. She also loved Psalm 139:13–14. Yes, they were all marvelously made, and Hannah needed them to know it.

As Hannah had finished writing the program just a few days ago, she thought about how much farther she may have been if she had gone through similar workshops. To be able to present, she'd borrowed a small projector from her church, and she continued to praise God because he was providing the manna just as He said He would. Hannah had to admit it felt good to walk in this level of obedience to the Lord.

"Alright, ladies, let's get started. I want you to begin with introducing yourself by sharing a positive affirmation about yourself.

You will fill in the paper I placed before you on your tables with a few affirmations that describe you. I want you to think about your personal strengths, things you have accomplished, and/or your positive qualities," Hannah said.

"*Umm,* what if you don't have either of those?" one of the older women at the far table asked.

Hannah attempted to read her name tag. "Ah, Ms. Joan, is it?"

"Yes, but you can just call me Joan."

"I'm going to continue to say Ms. out of respect, if you don't mind."

"Okay," Ms. Joan said, looking down at the table.

"Ms. Joan, are you from Pastor Dickerson's church?"

"Yes, I am."

"I thought so. As I was saying, We all have a strength, an accomplishment, or a positive quality. We have just taken on all of the negative words of others throughout our lives. I want you to think about what you are good at," Hannah continued, walking toward the table where the woman sat. She felt odd giving advice to one of her elders.

"I haven't had much time to be good at something in my life. I don't want to do this," Ms. Joan continued. Hannah could tell she was only pretending to be tough. She sensed sadness in the woman.

"Well, I tell you what, Ms. Joan, why don't you just listen as the others share, and then you can jump in if you'd like. If not, no pressure. Will that work?" The woman didn't respond, and she jerked away as Hannah lay her hand on her shoulder, so she quickly removed it. *Lord, help me to help Ms. Joan,* Hannah prayed in her heart.

Just then, she looked up and saw her mom enter. Hannah's mouth dropped when she saw her carrying a large pan with a huge bowl on top of it. There were also a few extra bags hanging from her arm. Her mom mouthed, "I brought food." The other women looked up, whispering about what was in the containers. Her mom was off and had surprised her again with lunch for her and the women. Hannah loved her mom's cooking. She turned to grab one of the bags her mom was struggling with. She then turned after hearing someone else enter. It was her Aunt Loretta. Her aunt had helped out all last week. Today was not her day to volunteer, so Hannah was a little surprised to see her.

Things were still a little awkward between the two of them, so they didn't say much to each other.

As her mom began to unwrap what she'd brought to serve, Hannah headed back inside the main meeting space to quickly give the women instructions on how to complete their affirmation sheets. She answered a few clarifying questions and reminded Ms. Joan that it was okay if hers was left blank.

She then returned to find out if she could help with serving. The aroma from the containers made her stomach growl. She attempted to peek inside the large pan covered with aluminum foil, but her mom lightly smacked her hand.

"You will wait, missy."

"I just wanted to see what you brought," Hannah said.

"I have grilled chicken wraps, broccoli cheddar soup, and one of my homemade pound cakes."

"Dang, Mama. When did you cook all this?"

"I started working on it last night. I wanted to serve the women again. I would love to come every Monday as I can. I'm sorry I'm a little past lunchtime. I see you've started your afternoon workshop already."

"It's okay. They can take a break to eat, and we will get back to it afterward. Thanks for coming over to help out. You didn't have to come on the day you don't volunteer," Hannah said, turning to face her Aunt Loretta, who stood off to the side looking down at a message on her phone. She seemed fearful of whatever she was reading but quickly changed her facial expression before looking up and responding.

"It's no problem. I don't mind. I really want to make things up to you."

"Is everything okay, Aunt Loretta?" Hannah asked, noticing another message pop up on her aunt's phone. Her aunt ignored it this time and stuffed her phone in her pants pocket, but her hands were trembling.

"Yeah. Just trying to find my own place. That was another text message about an apartment I checked into. Everything is getting so expensive. I'm exhausted from looking."

Hannah didn't buy her aunt's response, but she left it alone and said, "Well, thanks again."

"Alright. Let's go serve the ladies," Hannah's mom said, handing the paper plates to her aunt and grabbing the large pan. Hannah grabbed the bowl and led the way back into the small meeting space.

After lunch, Hannah was stuffed, but she had to finish the workshop. Her mom and aunt remained as she asked the women to begin introducing themselves using the positive affirmations they'd created earlier. Ms. Joan remained silent. Hannah's heart went out to the woman. She wondered what she'd been through. After the introductions, Hannah walked the women through goal setting. She walked around to assist as they wrote out their goals.

Hannah noticed an unusual sadness in her aunt's eyes as she glanced up at her. *What's really going on with her?* Hannah wondered. Her mom patted her aunt's hand as they continued sitting quietly, observing Hannah interacting with the women.

Once the women seemed to be done with their goals, Hannah asked for volunteers to share.

Amara, one of the women from House of Hope raised her hand. "My goals are simple. I want to do better for myself."

After Amara shared, most of the other women nodded in agreement. Hannah thanked her for sharing.

She then asked her try and be more specific.

"What do you mean?" asked Amara.

"I mean, what do you plan to do specifically to better yourself?" Hannah asked.

"Okay."

"Those are some of the things we will focus on in our empowerment workshops. I have some speakers and trainers I've reached out to in order to help you develop a solid plan, but I don't want you to just develop a plan. Remember, we are here to equip you, but we need to know what kind of assistance and training you all might need."

At those words, Hannah glanced at her aunt again who now had tears in her eyes. She looked at Hannah and whispered, "I'm so sorry. I'm proud of you."

Hannah choked back tears. Her anger seeming to dissipate for the first time since learning of her aunt's situation. She felt her aunt's pain.

Maybe it's her lack of self-worth that is causing her to tear up. That may have been the reason she stayed with Malcolm for so long, a man who wouldn't keep a job. Hannah still couldn't wrap her mind around it. As a kid, she'd admired her aunt's drive and success. *What happened to her?*

Her mom pulled her aunt into an embrace as they sat. Hannah wanted to move closer to her, but her feet wouldn't move to hug her. She had missed and still loved her aunt, but she didn't know if she was ready to reconcile with her. Sure, she could help out at the center.

She actually had been doing a great job, but Hannah didn't know if she could let her guard down just yet, so she did her best not to focus on Aunt Loretta and called on the next woman to share her goals.

By the end of the workshop, Hannah was emotionally exhausted. Many of the women knew what they wanted, but their barriers of past brokenness caused them to struggle to see their way out, which hindered them from setting goals and coming up with their own affirmations.

Lord, there is a lot of work for you to do here. I know I can't do this alone. And heal the broken places in Aunt Loretta's life. Help her to live passed her divorce. I pray she doesn't return to that man's lies and manipulation. Reveal her value to her.

CHAPTER THIRTEEN

Friday, March 26

Nearly another month had passed, and the center was operating in a greater capacity than Hannah could have imagined. After having a few minutes to log into her computer and look over the business PayPal account, she noticed they had gotten in more funding through online donations, but they weren't a lot.

I wonder why I haven't been getting the alerts like I was before. I'll have to check it out later. Lord, there is just not enough time to do everything. Because she still wasn't receiving a salary from the center as of yet, she and Levi were a little strapped for cash. They were on a strict budget, so Hannah could only eat out once a week, and her shopping was limited to necessities only, but it was all worth it. Hannah had no regrets, other than the extra hours she had to spend at the center, but it couldn't be helped. In addition, she prayed the online donations would increase as they were when she first opened because they could help with various expenses and things like marketing. She had paid six months toward the lease upfront, so it was a must to keep getting in funding to help with events and other smaller fees. Most of the remaining grant money would pay for the lease and utilities. She enjoyed pouring into the women and seeing their lives change little by little, so she would keep walking by faith.

"Tonight's Creative Purpose event is going to be amazing," Hannah said, hugging Tamela.

She thanked her for helping out with most of the details for this event. Hannah was grateful Tamela and her Aunt Loretta continued to be consistent volunteers. Despite her aunt's personal issues, none of her help at the center had gone unnoticed, so Hannah planned to give her and Tamela a small token of appreciation this evening. She would give Mama Jefferson her gift tomorrow morning when she, Levi, and Ariel headed over to her house for breakfast.

"Is there anything else needing to be done before the women begin arriving?" Aunt Loretta asked, rearranging the tables for the event.

"I don't think so. Mama is going to be here with the refreshments once she goes home and changes her clothes. April is five minutes away. If we forgot something, it will get done as we go about the night."

"Got it," Aunt Loretta said.

Hannah stepped outside to grab the paint, brushes, and canvases that had been donated from a local art store. As she was closing her trunk, she noticed a black car. As she looked closer, she realized it was the same one she'd seen driving by on Wednesday. Not knowing if the person was connected to one of the women who came and went all the time, she decided she would call and ask for periodic police patrol of the area. The person pulled off again when they noticed Hannah watching. *That better not be Malcolm.*

When she returned inside, she told the volunteers to be careful and call the police if they saw anything suspicious. She gave them the description of the black car and told them they would all leave together from now on. They all agreed. She watched her aunt to see if she would give a hint of it possibly being her husband, but she didn't act strange at all.

With the time nearing for tonight's event, Hannah then instructed Tamela to grab the writing prompts for the creative writing section from her office desk and Aunt Loretta to set up the mic and stool Hannah had borrowed from their church.

Hannah's phone pinged. She pulled her cell phone from her back pocket and read the message she'd received from Pastor Isaiah Carter, the lead pastor of one of the churches the center served, Mount Bethel Missionary Baptist Church. He was letting her know their church had sent an online donation of five hundred dollars through PayPal. Hannah sent a quick thank you and began to tuck her phone back into her pocket. It pinged again.

She read the message: *Let me know if you got it.* Hannah told him she would let him know after the event she was getting ready to host.

His message lifted her spirits. *Yes, that's at least one larger online donation. Thank You, Lord. Keep them coming.*

They had just finished setting up before the first set of women started arriving. April greeted the women at the door, asking them which section they would like to sit in based on talent. Hannah loved April. She was one of the sweetest people she'd ever met, even if she couldn't be consistent. They hadn't been friends as long as she and Tamela, but she had been nothing but a blessing to Hannah. She was grateful to have both of her friends helping her out.

April's bright smile seemed to cause the women to respond with joy and even hugs. As the main meeting room began to fill up, Hannah noticed Ms. Joan at the door. The older woman looked at April with a frown, but Hannah had already warned her friend about Ms. Joan. April continued smiling at Ms. Joan as Hannah headed over to the door.

"Hey, Ms. Joan. How about we try you at the song writing/poetry table?"

"Okay, I guess," the older woman said, seeming more comfortable in Hannah's presence.

"Alright. Why don't you take a seat right here?" Hannah said, pulling out a chair at the table toward the back of the room for Ms. Joan to sit.

"Thank you," Ms. Joan mumbled.

"You're welcome. If you need anything, ask one of the volunteers to come get me."

"Okay," Ms. Joan replied before Hannah hurried away to the front to get them started.

"Alright, ladies. Thank you so much for being here this evening. This center would not be able to operate without the women of this community who are being impacted already by what we are doing here. Well, tonight we are going to have some fun."

"Yay," a few of the women cheered.

"We are going to do something called Creative Purpose. This is simply the belief in one's ability to generate creative ideas, solutions to problems, and express yourselves creatively. In other words, to tap into the creativity that God has placed within you. Now, you have already been seated in the area where you feel you are creative. We have song writing/poetry at the back table, the creative writers over to my left, and those who will try their hand at art here in the middle."

"Oh, Lord help, I don't know how to write songs or poems," Amara said from the back of the room.

Giggles spread across the room. Hannah waited for everyone to settle before she continued.

"It's okay, Amara. Tonight is not about being perfect, but using creativity to build our confidence and to attempt to identify our gifts and purpose. You are more than welcome to move to another area," Hannah said.

"No, I'll try it out," Amara replied.

"Good. So we will begin by each of you introducing yourself and telling us one creative hobby or interest you may have or once had."

"Okay," a few women stated.

After the introductions were complete, Hannah returned to the front and gave the next instruction.

She explained that the women at the canvases would have thirty minutes to create a piece of simple art using the template provided. The groups at the writing tables would create a short story or an outline for their memoir and write out the first page of it using the themes and instructions provided. Finally, the song writing/poetry group would free write songs or poems based on what was on their heart at the moment. Hannah set a timer, then she and the volunteers helped her mom pass out the refreshments.

Once she called time, Hannah couldn't believe her eyes. Most of the women continued for another ten minutes before looking up. She then said, "Alright, ladies. Who will be brave enough to share?"

Hands flew up all around the room, including Ms. Joan. Hannah was amazed and called on her first. "Come on up here, Ms. Joan. You can either read your poem or sing the lyrics to your song if you would like."

Hannah just knew coming to the front of the room would be a *no* for Ms. Joan, but the woman stood and walked proudly up front. The entire room looked on with anticipation. Hannah assumed Ms. Joan would read the words to the song she wrote, but when she began to sing it, Hannah nearly fell over. Ms. Joan had a beautiful alto range voice.

"I feel the peace of Christ again. I know with him somehow I'll win and not lose...I'm free in Thee.

My hope was lost but now it's found. My feet are back on solid ground...I'll win somehow..." Ms. Joan sang over and over as if her only audience was Christ. Hannah, the volunteers, and the other women cheered. By the time, she had finished, Ms. Joan's face was streaked with tears, but she opened her eyes and smiled, thanking everyone for their kindness as they continued to cheer. Next, she thanked Hannah for doing the activity. She loved it.

Hannah stepped to the front and asked who would like to go next, and her aunt raised her hand. Hannah looked around for others, but God was tugging at her heart to call on her Aunt Loretta. As her aunt took the mic, Hannah stepped back next to her mom who whispered, "Thank you for giving her a chance."

Her aunt stood there holding the mic for a few seconds before she spoke. "Good evening, ladies." Her voice trembled. "I'm so glad to be here this evening. I decided I wanted to participate as well. I wrote a chapter from what would be my memoir. If I were to write a memoir, it would be entitled *Extinguished Light*."

One of the women in the crowd replied, "Wow. That's deep."

"Yes, it is. I had to dig deep and really deal with me. I did a quick outline and wrote out the first couple of pages of what could be one of the chapters. I would title this chapter 'A Time of Darkness.' I wrote it as if I were reliving it, so here it goes: *I feel trapped. I'm in a place where I feel I can't get out.*

This man is the worse. I have put up with his foolishness long enough—too long. I thought he loved me, but he keeps saying such ugly words to me, 'Who else is going to marry you? You're not even that cute. I only stayed this long because you take care of me.' Then, he laughs and later says, 'You know I don't mean what I say.' But he does mean what he says, and I've been his fool."

Hannah gasped. "That's crazy," she whispered to her mom.

"I know. Keep listening."

Her aunt continued, *"I can't believe I didn't notice the signs of manipulation. How can I call myself a mental health counselor? How can I continue to help anyone else? I didn't even believe my niece when she told me about Malcolm. Plus, I'm trained to notice certain signs of issues in people. There have been at least three more young ladies who have come forth over the years. This is all my fault. I should have reported him years ago. I've got to get out, but he keeps telling me that I will be arrested as well. The last girl's mom pressed charges, and he keeps saying he'll tell the police that I knew about it if he gets arrested, but I didn't know. God knows I didn't know, but it's just as bad blaming those girls and telling them all they were lying and they were too fast.*

"I deserve this. I feel awful. It's no wonder my niece doesn't want anything to do with me. My sister tells me she is doing well, but I feel awful for how I treated her. I wouldn't blame her if she never spoke to me again. I just need the courage to leave. I've already filed the divorce papers. I have to find a way to get away from this man. I must do this now. He continues to spend the money in our savings account and even the money for our bills. I'll call my sister, Tamika, and see if I can stay with her until the divorce is finalized. He can have the house. Let him figure out how to pay the bills on his own. I have two degrees. I can come out of retirement and pick up some clients and even get a part time job if I have to. With me gone, he might get and keep a job. I just want out.

"I once was a vibrant woman with so much going for me. I graduated at the top of my class in high school and college, and I had a great career. I don't need him, so how did I allow him to dim my light? I fell in love, and I fell for his lies. Not only did he dim my light, he extinguished it. That's what he did, and it may never illuminate again. I have to get out—now."

After her aunt finished sharing, the room was silent minus the "wows" and the "my Lords" from the women, but Hannah was fuming. *What about those other girls? And she stayed with that evil man. I tried to tell her about that monster. She wants to leave him now that he's done more damage.* As her aunt walked back to her seat, Hannah tried to calm herself. Her aunt sobbed, but Hannah still couldn't move toward her. She just stared at her. Then, she closed her eyes and prayed for God to remove the rage she felt.

Give her grace, she heard in her spirit.

She took a few deep breaths, then opened her eyes again, but she still couldn't move.

The next thing she knew, several of the women had circled Aunt Loretta and began to pray for her. April held her aunt's hand, and Hannah's mom stood next to her. Many of the women cried and prayed for God to continue to move and to heal Aunt Loretta's heart, then, Hannah heard Ms. Joan singing her song.

"I feel the peace of Christ again. I know with Him somehow I'll win and not lose...I'm free in thee. My hope was lost, but now it's found. My feet are back on solid ground...I'll win somehow..."

They embraced one another tight, and Hannah's mom came over to her.

"I understand if you're not ready," her mom whispered.

"Mama, how could she stay with him? He hurt other girls," Hannah cried, laying her head on her mom's chest as Hannah's mom wrapped her arms around her.

"Lord, help me to forgive her completely and not to bring it up again."

She knew what God had instructed, but it was so hard to let go. Yes, Hannah loved her—that's what hurt so bad—but she just didn't know if she would see her in the role as her dear aunt again.

CHAPTER FOURTEEN

Saturday, March 27

Not having the time to look at the donations last night after the Creative Purpose event, Hannah wanted to finish breakfast for her family and head over to the center. Things were still on the upswing, and she wanted to get there to plan for which larger events she would be able to host. The first bake-off was coming up fast, and she wanted to review the budget for it.

Having gotten in a quick scripture journaling session at 5:30, she was now fully dressed and almost done cooking the bacon. Ariel sat at the table with her head resting on her arms and her eyes closed while she waited for her food. Hannah was a little grateful her daughter was not a morning person, so she could get in some silence before heading to the center. Feeling blessed by what God had been doing, Hannah hummed one of her favorite gospel tunes by Tasha Cobbs Leonard, "No Longer Slaves," as she lay the first few pieces of bacon on the napkins inside the plate next to the stove. As her humming turned into singing, she must have been too loud because Ariel called her name.

"Mommy, why are you singing so loud?" her daughter whined.

"I'm sorry, grumpy granny," Hannah said, giving her a kiss on the cheek, singing lower to her daughter. Ariel waved her away.

"Is the food ready yet?" Ariel whined.

"Yes, I'm making your plate now," Hannah said, then she continued singing.

"Alright. That's what I'm talking about," Levi said, joining in with the song and kissing Ariel on her forehead. "We are no longer slaves to fear." Levi started shouting like a Baptist preacher.

"You are such a clown," Hannah said, giggling.

"Daddyyy, you are tooooo loud," Ariel complained, covering her ears.

"Oh, sweetheart, I'm sorry. Why are you so grumpy this morning?" Levi asked, shaking Ariel's shoulders from side to side as if he was trying to get her to perk up.

"I want to eat and go back to bed."

"That would be a no. You can do that when you get to Aunt Brittany's," Levi said.

Ariel was spending the day with Hannah's sister to spend some time with her cousin Neveah, and this was Levi's Saturday to work.

"Whyyyy?" Ariel cried, wiping away her crocodile tears.

"You're going to have a great day, my Busy Bee," Levi sang, kissing their daughter on the forehead again.

"Daddyyyy," Ariel yelled.

Hannah laughed at her daughter and husband's interaction as she finished preparing the eggs. She loved how Levi tried to pull Ariel out of her grumpiness in the mornings, but her daughter wasn't having it, especially having to leave home so early on a Saturday.

"Babe, are you almost done? I'm going to have to take it with me."

"Yes. Everything is ready," Hannah said as he walked over and kissed her neck and side hugged her.

"I'll make a bacon and egg sandwich to eat in the car."

"I'll do it. Go finish getting ready," Hannah said, placing Ariel's plate in front of her.

After Levi was finished getting dressed, he grabbed his breakfast, kissed Hannah and Ariel again, and headed out the door. Hannah hurried Ariel along, and they were soon in the car on their way. By the time they made it to Brittany's, Ariel was still in a funk. Hannah walked her inside and remained with her for a few minutes before leaving.

"I've got her. You go ahead and do what you need to do today. TT's big girl will be just fine," Hannah's sister said. She felt sad as she pulled out of the parking lot, not liking to see her baby girl like that. Hannah said a prayer for Ariel. It made her feel a little better as she headed to the center. She'd do her best to be done by lunch time and would take Ariel out on a date. Just the two of them.

Heading inside, Hannah was excited about the other activities the board had helped her plan for the women. She hoped she had enough for the community success fair she planned in the coming months, and the bake-off, which was the first big event. She wanted to decorate with balloons and give away a few gift cards to the winners for their participation. Hannah sat in the main meeting space at the receptionist desk to finish pulling her plans together.

She wrote out how the day would go, step by step. She added who she would need assistance from and how the outside setup would look. She made a note to print a few more flyers that would be needed to put up around town. She had already begun sharing on social media. Then, she made a list of those she had received a definite yes from. At the thought of the fun they would have, Hannah giggled to herself, picturing her mom, Aunt Melissa, and the other mothers trash talking about who had the best baked goods.

Next, she wrote out the plan for the community success fair. This one would take more money to host. She wouldn't need a venue because she planned to host it around the parking lot with tables set up. She just had to get the other stores on board with her. Hannah would need to have a marketing and promotion budget. She would need to rent tables and chairs, and she would need to find out the fees the participants might charge. Hannah paused as she thought about how good this would do for the community.

I would love to have job recruiters who would interview and even do some hiring. I also want nurses here checking blood pressures and even glucose levels, and it would be great if an OB/GYN would come out and get the women signed up to get their yearly checkups.

She started giggling to herself again. *Lord, this is exciting.* Ooh, *what if we also got some college recruiters or trade schools to show up and tell the women their options on continuing their education? What if there was a night school director here? And even someone to help with finding income-based apartments.*

Hannah's thoughts were in overdrive, but she knew she had to choose because her budget couldn't afford to bring them all in unless they volunteered their time, which would be great, but wasn't likely.

She would make some calls to see if she could get some to come for free because it was a community outreach, so anyone could show up and participate, not just the women she served. More excited than ever, Hannah finished jotting down the details for the event and pulled up the bank account for the center. She didn't have a lot to work with because of the money needed for the overhead and utilities. *Let's see which community events we could do.*

She then pulled out the other notebook she kept with the running fees, payments, and expenses; opened her laptop; and logged into PayPal to see what else could be added to the budget. As Hannah reviewed the new online donations before transferring them from PayPal, she didn't see the five hundred dollars from Pastor Carter's church. *That's strange.* Maybe it didn't come through yet. She gave Pastor Carter a call. He checked his account and told her the money had cleared on his end.

Confused, Hannah said, "Did you send it through the link that's on the So That you May Live Facebook page?"

"Yes," he said.

"Oh, okay. Maybe I'm missing something. I'll text you back. Let me check the PayPal account again. Something could be going on because I didn't get the alert for your donation, but that's been happening lately."

"Okay. Just let me know you've got it. We are so proud of you."

"*Awww.* Thank you so much. I will call or text you once I check."

"Yes, ma'am," he said.

Hannah searched for Mount Bethel Missionary Baptist Church and the pastor's name. There was nothing there, nor was the five hundred dollars, and Hannah was still not understanding why she was no longer getting the alerts to her phone, but she found donations in the account when she logged in, so she checked the notifications settings.

How did they get turned off? Hannah wondered. *Okay, this is not making any sense. I didn't turn them off. Let me call PayPal. Maybe something is going on with their site.*

Hannah located their customer service number at the bottom of the account page. Grabbing her phone, she dialed the number, indicated that she wanted to speak to a live customer service rep, and waited. Hannah put her phone on speaker and put away some supplies she'd ordered as she waited.

After several minutes, someone answered, "Thank you for calling PayPal. This is Stephanie. Can I have your name?" The rep finished asking her the other account information to verify her identity. "How may I help you?" the woman on the other end said.

"Yes, I'm having trouble viewing all of my donations for my women's center business PayPal account."

"I'm not sure if I understand what you're asking."

"Okay, let me start over. I've been receiving online donations through my business PayPal account, and I'm not seeing one that was just sent yesterday."

"Do you think the person may have typed in your email incorrectly when they were donating?" asked the woman.

"No. He said it had cleared on his end."

"That means you should see it on your side."

"But I don't," Hannah said. "I'm looking at the list of donations on the main page where you find the balance."

"Let me check it. I'm going to place you on a brief hold."

"Okay," Hannah said, beyond confused now.

After a few minutes, the woman returned to the line. "Ah, Mrs. Jefferson, I see here where you deleted a five-hundred-dollar donation and other donation amounts from the archive."

"Excuse me. I didn't delete anything from this account."

"Are you sure?"

"I'm positive. I know I've been super busy around here, but I know I didn't delete receipts of donations. Why would I do that?"

"Let me put you on another brief hold. I'm still checking your account," the representative said.

"Okay," Hannah said, standing and pacing, her nerves getting the best of her. *Lord, have I been hacked and didn't know it?*

"Mrs. Jefferson?"

"I'm here."

"Yes, as I said. There have been several listed donations deleted from your list over several weeks. They total about $5,000. This was all done while logged in with your credentials."

"What? How?"

"They were for different amounts."

"What name was it?"

"It appears to be to a woman named Cassandra Lee."

"I have never sent money to anybody with that name. I have no clue who that might be," Hannah explained.

"Mrs. Jefferson, it sounds like someone may have gained access to your account information somehow, and they have been sending payments to this person."

"How? I just said I don't know that name, Hannah said, fuming.

"In order to delete anything, a person has to be able to get into the account."

"Could the account have been hacked?"

"We would have to further investigate, but hackers don't normally leave some of the money in the account. They take it all. Does anyone have your log-in info?"

"Not that I know of."

"It appears they accessed it somehow and may have turned off the alerts."

"I'm sorry, but this is not making sense to me," Hannah said.

"I understand. Mrs. Jefferson, we will do a little more digging, and you will get the results between fourteen to thirty days. Most take no more than fourteen days.

"Okay. Am I guaranteed I'll get the money back?"

"I can't answer that right now," the woman said.

"Do I need to file a police report?"

"I would encourage you to do so, but they may need our information before they can do a full investigation. For the time being, I would advise you to change your username and password for this account, and set up a two-step verification to make it more difficult for someone to get into it."

"I will do that now," Hannah mumbled, trying to stifle her tears.

"I am so sorry this happened to you, Ms. Jefferson. You will hear from us soon."

"Thank you," Hannah said before disconnecting the call.

She lay her head on the table and sobbed. She couldn't even consider calling Pastor Carter back and telling him she couldn't find his donation because it appeared someone had stolen it, along with several others. "This is too much. I'm not set up to deal with this kind of craziness. I think I moved too fast opening the center, Lord. How am I supposed to handle this? People have trusted me enough to donate to us," Hannah cried.

A few minutes later, Tamela came through the door.

"Hannah, what's wrong?"

She lifted her head and looked at her friend, tears streaming, "Tam, someone has taken donations—about $5,000—from the PayPal account. I don't know what I'm going to do. This looks bad, really bad."

"What? I'm so sorry to hear this. Did you call PayPal?"

"Yes. I just got off the phone with them, They said it looks like I did it. The rep said it appeared I've been sending money to someone named Cassandra Lee. I don't know anyone by that name. She said the person may have gotten access to my username and password somehow."

"That's awful," Tamela said, standing and handing Hannah tissue from the table at the back of the main meeting space. "Sis, I'm here for you."

"Thank you. I really appreciate it. This business stuff is so stressful. How can I tell supporters that their donations have been stolen?"

"You have to, but it's not your fault."

"But I should have been more careful. I should have been monitoring more closely, but I've just been so busy."

"It's going to be okay, sis."

"Girl, I just don't know how someone could have gotten my information and why they would do this. I also have to file a police report. This is crazy. I can't do this."

"Wait a minute," Tamela said, a confused look on her face.

"What?" Hannah asked.

"Now, I'm not trying to say anything about your Aunt Loretta. I love her and how she has helped the women here at the center, but I saw her coming out of your office at the end of the Creative Purpose event, and that wasn't the first time. I've seen her a few more times before, but I didn't think anything of it because we are both often helping all over the center."

"Huh?"

"Yes. That night, I saw her come out when I ran inside to use the restroom. She said she was taking something in there for you, but I heard her on the phone with someone, and she said something about giving them some money, but it sounded like her and the person were arguing. That's when you and your mom were outside talking with a few of the other ladies who were still here. I didn't think anything about it until you just mentioned someone having your information.

"I'm not believing what I'm hearing. We have our differences, but I can't see her taking from me, and who is Cassandra Lee? How is my aunt connected to her?" Hannah said, thinking out loud.

"Your things are always in your office, right?" asked Tamela.

"Yes. I leave my phone and my laptop in there when I'm hosting workshops in here, but I don't keep my log-in info out for just anyone to grab. I didn't have it sitting out anywhere."

"You think she could have gotten a hold of it somehow?" Tamela asked.

"I don't think so. And even if she did, where is the money being sent, and how does she know them?"

"Maybe her husband is behind it," Tamela said. "You did say he was evil."

"He is, but I still can't see my aunt doing this to me," Hannah said, growing silent and thinking.

She thought back to the terrified look on her aunt's face when she received those text messages and how strange she acted. Then, the black car she'd been seeing came back to her. *Could that really be Malcolm? Has he been following her? She wouldn't let him talk her into stealing from me, would she? But how? What about this Cassandra character? Is it someone connected to Malcolm?* She grew more and more confused. Hannah closed her laptop and packed her things into her bag.

"I've got to get to the bottom of this," Hannah said, standing and pulling her bag onto her shoulder.

"I can stay here and work on something until you get back."

"No, that's okay," Hannah said, on high alert now. It may or may not be her aunt, so she wasn't taking any chances.

"Are you sure?" Tamela asked. "I'm here now. I can get something done so you won't be so far behind."

"Yes, I'm sure. I apologize, but I'm just going to go ahead and lock up."

"I understand, sis," Tamela said, leaning in to hug Hannah.

"I know your time is precious," Hannah said. "I'm sorry you had to drive over for nothing."

The safest thing Hannah felt she could do was lock up if she wasn't going to be there. She had to be more attentive, which she should have been doing from the beginning, but something like this happening never crossed her mind. Tamela was her close friend and had never given her a reason not to trust her, but her own aunt may have stolen some of the money that funded the center, and that unnerved her at the moment.

No, I can't take any more chances, Hannah said to herself.

"God will provide what was lost," Tamela said, hugging Hannah.

Hannah sat in her car for a few more minutes thinking through the past month or so. "Now that I think about it, during that event, Aunt Loretta talked about Malcolm threatening to report that she knew about what he was doing to those girls. Maybe he has been blackmailing her for money some kind of way. But it may not be her. It could be someone else."

The center is my responsibility. How could I be so careless? What is the board going to think? What is Pastor Carter going to think? I have to tell him the money has been stolen. Lord, why? she thought, sitting up and turning the ignition. As she pulled away, Hannah tried to remember any other times she had left her computer unattended without logging out and her phone on her desk. There were several because she was always running around making sure every area was covered, but she had people there she could trust—at least that's what she believed. *But how could the person have gotten my username and password? I have it stored in my contacts, and only I can unlock my phone. This is not happening. Why is this happening?*

CHAPTER FIFTEEN

Saturday, March 27

As Hannah drove to her mother's apartment to ask her aunt about what Tamela had just shared with her, Hannah sobbed. She was annoyed and was ready to let it all go. Arriving at her mom's place, Hannah got out the car and headed to the door. Hannah prayed for guidance. She rang the doorbell and waited.

Aunt Loretta opened the door. "Hey. How are you?" her aunt said.

"Not so good, Auntie. I need to talk to you."

"Hannah? What are you doing here? I thought you were at the center working on some things," her mom said from the couch. She was stretched out watching T.V., still in her pajamas.

"Hey, Mama. I'm done at the center. I came by to talk to Auntie about something," Hannah said, walking over to sit beside her mom.

"Why do you look like you've been crying?" her mom asked.

"I have been. It appears that someone has been stealing donations from the center using the PayPal account."

"Oh, no. How did you find out?" her mom asked.

"Because a pastor reached out to me yesterday during the Creative Purpose event and told me he had just donated five hundred dollars. I didn't get a chance to look at the account last night to let him know I got it, but I did today. I couldn't find it, so I called PayPal to find out what was going on because the notifications had been turned off too, but I didn't turn them off, so I thought something was going on with their site. Well, the representative said some donations had been transferred to the account of a lady named Cassandra Lee, then the person deleted them, so I wouldn't find out."

"What?" Aunt Loretta said with a shocked expression.

"Auntie," Hannah said, turning to face Aunt Loretta, "I wanted to ask you about something Tamela shared with me."

"What is it?"

"She said she saw you coming out of my office while the rest of us were outside talking last night. Did you do this, Auntie? Maybe for Malcolm?"

"No," her aunt said. "I would never do anything like that to you, not for Malcolm, not for anyone," she said, bursting into tears. "And I don't know any Cassandras."

"Why are you crying?" Hannah asked.

"I just want us to make amends and let go of everything from the past."

"She also said you were arguing with someone about money and having to find yourself somewhere to stay," Hannah added, ignoring her aunt's comment.

Her aunt hesitated several seconds before speaking. Hannah watched as she wringed her hands in her lap, and Hannah noticed that fearful look again. "Yeah. I was arguing with Malcolm."

"Really? Why?" Hannah asked, her voice elevating.

"Okay, enough of this," her mom said. "You know Loretta didn't steal any money from you, Hannah."

"About my money from my retirement funds," her aunt said, interrupting Hannah's mom's scolding. "and the money I've invested over the years that he couldn't access because I took his name off of the accounts, and he's just finding out."

"So, Tamela is only telling the truth about some of what she told me?" Hannah asked.

"Yes. I was not inside your office."

"Auntie, you did just admit he is harassing you about money. Why should I believe that he didn't talk you into taking from the center?"

"You don't have to, but it's the truth."

"Has he also been following you? Is that who is in the black car I keep seeing outside of the center?" Her aunt hesitated again. "Auntie, please answer me."

"He has been...but I told you I didn't do this."

"What? How did he find you? It's not like Mama is living in the same place."

"I don't know. I just want to be left alone. He keeps telling me he's going to kill me if I don't give him my money, the money I worked hard for all these years. That's why he still hasn't signed the divorce papers."

"Loretta, you need to go to the police and file a restraining order," Hannah's mom said.

"He's just talking," her aunt said.

"Auntie, you need to listen to Mama. She can go with you."

"Why can't he just leave me alone?"

"Because he's a user and abuser," Hannah said.

"Hannah," her mom said.

"What, Mama? It's the truth."

"Did PayPal tell you anything else?" her mom asked, changing the subject.

"No. They are investigating a little further, and I have to file a police report."

"And what about the other volunteers? Didn't you say Tamela is there all the time helping out? Could she be trying to set up Loretta?"

"Mama, Tam is my closest friend, and she loves Aunt Loretta. She has no reason to lie. Auntie just admitted that she was arguing with him on the phone."

"And your aunt just told you that she wasn't in your office. The argument was about her money."

"You may think it's me because of your experience with me, but I promise you I did not take from you. I would never do that to you, not for Malcolm, not for anyone," Aunt Loretta said, coming to sit next to Hannah. "I love you, Hannah, and I just want us to put all of the past behind us."

"Auntie, I know you do, but it's just hard for me to let go of how you treated me in the past, and I don't put anything past him."

"I know, and I'm sorry. That's why I love what you are doing now. I wish I would have been brave enough to leave him back then."

"I'm sorry, Auntie, for going with Tamela's word right away. I will wait until the investigation is finished and will be more cautious of Tamela and the other volunteers from now on. But I won't be able to use you at the center any longer. I'm just not comfortable with what you just told me about his threats and him following you, and you shouldn't be comfortable either. I want you and the other women at the center to be safe. Please consider getting a restraining order. Mama or I can go with you."

"I will consider it," Aunt Loretta said, tears forming in her eyes. "And I understand your concerns. I truly love being around those women and helping them when and where I can."

"I know you do," Hannah said. "Thank you for all of your help. Maybe, with the restraining order, it will keep him away from you, and you could come back."

"I hate this is happening to the both of you," her mom said, leaning over to hug Hannah and then standing to hug Aunt Loretta.

"Me too," Hannah said, standing to leave. "I will talk to you two later."

"I love you," her mom said, standing to give her a bear hug.

"I love you too, Mama."

As she headed to the door, she could still hear her aunt crying, and Hannah fought back her own tears. She turned and headed back towards her aunt. Hannah wrapped her arms around Aunt Loretta's shoulders as she sat with her head bowed, tears flowing. Hannah couldn't hold back her own tears. She cried and held her aunt. She had missed her being a part of her life.

"Auntie, God loves you. He made you to do amazing things. You don't have to keep dealing with that jerk. He has broken your spirit the way he broke mine all those years ago. God can heal you the way He healed me. You deserve better. You are better. You are better than the way he has treated and manipulated you."

Her aunt cried even more. Hannah's mom held her aunt's hand as Hannah was led to pray for her.

She couldn't stand to see the woman she had once looked up to so broken and lost, but Hannah knew better than anyone that God could mend her aunt's wounded heart.

CHAPTER SIXTEEN

Sunday, March 28

On Sunday following a much-needed time at church, Hannah and Ariel met up with her sister and niece at Pepperoni Palace Playhouse to allow the girls to play and to try to take her mind off of meeting with the board on Tuesday and what Pastor Carter would say once she told him the money was stolen. She also wanted time to catch up with her sister. They had both been working long hours, and she missed their chats and how they encouraged each other.

As she pulled into the parking lot, she was relieved it wasn't overcrowded. Opening the back door, she attempted to wake Ariel as she sat in her car seat, head back and mouth open, fast asleep. Hannah shook her daughter's shoulder, and she sat up with a frown.

"Come on, big girl. We're here. Let's go see Aunt Brittany and Neveah."

"Noooo," Ariel grunted, returning her head to the same position.

"Ariel, come on," Hannah said a little sterner this time.

"But, Mommy, I'm tired. I don't want to go."

"Ariel, Mommy doesn't have time for this. Come on. Your aunt is probably inside waiting for us."

Ariel finally sat up, stretched her arms above her head, and climbed out of her car seat. Hannah grabbed her hand as she finally got out of the car. As Ariel leaned on Hannah's leg, Hannah scanned the parking lot for her sister's metallic blue Ford Focus. She spotted it a few rows down closer to the entrance. Hannah walked slowly to the door with Ariel dragging her feet at her side. Excited to see her niece and thanking the older man who held the door open, Hannah moved as quickly past him as Ariel would allow, beaming as she walked toward her sister. Brittany knelt to hug and kiss Ariel.

Hannah leaned down to hug and kiss her niece, Neveah, holding her tight as if years had passed since she'd last seen her, but it had only been a few days.

"TT, you're squeezing me," Neveah said.

"It's because I love you so much," Hannah said, standing and stepping forward to hug and kiss her sister. "I still can't believe she is in kindergarten."

"You mean, she is almost out of kindergarten," Brittany said.

"You're right. She and Ariel are growing too fast."

Yes, they are," Brittany said, wrapping her arms around Hannah who couldn't pay the cashier fast enough before her niece started pulling her toward the playground area. "Hold on, Veah. We have to put our things at the booth first."

"Hurry, Mommy and TT. I want to play," Neveah said.

Ariel was still a little cranky after her nap in the car. Brittany giggled at the frown on Ariel's face.

"What's the matter with TT's big girl?"

"I want to go to bed."

"You don't want to play with your cousin?"

"Noooo," Ariel grunted, leaning into Hannah's right leg again.

"Ariel, Mommy needs to find a table and sit down, then you can put your head on the table or lay on my lap if you're still tired, but I'm sure Neveah would love to play with you."

"Yes, Ariel. Let's play," Neveah shouted above the laughter and other hustle and bustle around them.

"Not right now," Ariel said, whining softly, her eyes narrowing as she looked away.

Hannah and Brittany found a booth right next to the play area, and they sat down for a few minutes to chat, giving Ariel time to rest. Neveah grabbed Ariel's hand to head to the play area. Ariel snatched away and lay her head back down on her jacket on the table next to Hannah. Neveah tried again with no luck.

"Veah, give your little cousin a few minutes to rest. You go ahead and play," Brittany said.

"O...kay," Neveah said with a hint of sadness in her voice. She then hurried over to the jungle gym only a few steps away. A few seconds later, Hannah heard her niece giggle as she climbed up behind another little girl who seemed to be around her age. That's one of the things she loved about her niece.

She never met a stranger.

She is such a sweetheart, Hannah thought as she and Brittany kept their eyes on her as they began to chat.

"Girl, I needed this," Hannah said.

"Me too. I wish I didn't have such long work hours."

"Are you ready to paint some kiddie faces next Saturday?"

"You know I wouldn't miss my little miracle niece's fourth birthday party."

"I just can't believe she's turning four already," Hannah said.

"And I can't believe it either."

"Her party is going to be great. I haven't got many parents to RSVP, but that's okay. She just needs a few friends to hang out with."

"Agreed," Brittany said. "By the way, I still can't believe someone stole money from the center. And Tamela telling you she saw Auntie coming out of your office... I can't see Auntie doing that."

"Me either," said Hannah. "I mean, we have been estranged, but I just don't think she would do that.

"I hate that. I pray you find out who did it," Brittany said.

"Me too. Ah, man, Brit. I'm so stressed with all of this. I already had to jump through hoops to get the grant money we received because I'm a new nonprofit. Then, for somebody to steals five grand of the donations. I don't know if this entrepreneur stuff is for me."

"Don't give up, sis. It's hard, but I believe it will all work out."

"I hope so," Hannah said. "Not to mention, this puts me right back to handling more at the center with Aunt Loretta not being there, but with him following her, I couldn't chance it with the other women."

"I understand," her sister said. "What did Auntie say?"

"She understood."

"That's good to hear. I'm glad you two are working things out."

"Me too. I still struggle with the past, but as a believer now, I had to forgive her."

"I know it wasn't easy."

"It wasn't, but God kept speaking to my heart about showing her grace. Well, he said to show both her and Malcolm grace, but I'm still struggling a little with that one."

"Listen, I understand, but ask God to help you release him as well."

"Trust me, I have been praying."

"Well, I will join you in prayer.

"Thanks, sis," said Hannah. "Oh, by the way, are you going to be able to make it to the bake-off I'm trying to pull together to raise more funds?

"Yes. I was able to take off."

"Thank you." Hannah smiled. "I could really use the help, and I can't wait for you to meet the women and hang out with me. How are things with Travis and his parents?"

"Great. He is a totally different person now. He has matured even more since the last time you saw him. He's a great dad to Neveah."

"That's good to hear. You know I continue to pray for my niece to have her dad in her life. I'm glad he is finally getting it together. I think it's very important for them to have a relationship. I don't know how well I would have done if Daddy wasn't there for me growing up," Hannah said. "Even now as an adult, he has helped me through more things than I could have ever imagined."

"At least you have your dad. I still haven't heard from mine since him and Mama divorced, and I don't know if he's ever reached out to Malik," Brittany said.

"So, you understand how important it is?" Hannah asked.

"Absolutely.

"Speaking of Malik, have you heard from our brother at all?"

"No, not in a few months. He calls me every blue moon, and he doesn't stay on long."

"Same for me. Wow, that's crazy, Brit. Was Malik so angry with Mama back then that he hasn't reached out to us more?"

"It seems that way, but you have to admit Mama was a mess back then. Can you blame his anger?"

"No. You know it took us both a while to even forgive her. I want to at least know that he is okay," Hannah added.

"Me too."

"I wonder how things are going for him in the Marines. Do you realize we really don't know much more about our own brother? It's like he detached himself from us. We've experienced a lot of broken relationships," Hannah shared. "I really want him and Mama to reconnect. I can see the sadness in her eyes when she brings him up sometimes."

"I think God is mending this distance between our family. First, it was us and Mama. Now, it's you and Aunt Loretta, and soon it will be Mama and Malik," said Brittany.

"I pray that happens," said Hannah.

"It will. You think Auntie just showing wasn't God's doing?"

"I'm sure it was."

"I will try calling Malik when I get home."

"Sounds good," said Hannah.

At that moment, Ariel lifted her head. She eyed Hannah as if she was trying to remember where they were. "Are you ready to go play now?" Hannah asked.

Her daughter nodded. Hannah stood to let Ariel out of the booth, keeping an eye on her every move. As she and her sister continued talking, Hannah was grateful for the distraction. She and Brittany ordered a pizza and some wings and talked about old times. Yes, this was temporary, but for now it would do.

CHAPTER SEVENTEEN

Wednesday, April 1

After telling Pastor Carter about the stolen donation money on yesterday and meeting with the board on Monday, Hannah was more discouraged than before. Pastor Carter wanted her to return the funds to his church, not liking what he was hearing. Hannah apologized over and over and broke down in tears. Then, she returned his donation, using her own personal money. Pastor Carter let her know he would keep her and the situation in prayer.

During the board meeting, the accountant, Aubrey, made sly comments about how she needed to be more careful with the money people had trusted her with, and even Pastor Gibson had scolded her about not being able to run and grow a ministry if she didn't use more wisdom. At first, Hannah was upset at their words, but she knew they were right. They hadn't said anything different from what she had thought about herself. She didn't know why God had entrusted her with such a vision, and she had not been a good steward over it. Overall, the board had agreed she should keep the plans in place and go forward with the fundraisers and other events to replenish the funds because the continuous donations would help keep the center afloat because most of the grant money was going to the lease and utilities, and it was about time to pay the next six months on the lease. They had prayed with her and also encouraged her to keep documentation of the PayPal investigation and the police report for their records. She knew she was responsible for the donations, so she needed to do everything possible to try and get it back. Her credibility was on the line.

The most encouraging words came from Pastor Dickerson: "Our God is a big God," he'd said. "He's got you. Don't fear. Stay the course."

As she considered walking away from it all, Hannah received an email reply from her former principal letting her know she wouldn't be going after her for abandonment of contract. She felt that was a sign to start looking for teacher-related positions just in case she needed one. Hannah's husband, Levi, and Ms. Priscilla did their best to encourage her to not give up on the vision God had given to her, but for the past two days, she had searched for positions. She'd even updated her résumé and sent it out to a few positions she thought she would enjoy doing—just in case. Hannah knew that was her faith wavering once again, but she seriously considering walking away. Hannah had repented for her wavering heart numerous times just today, but she couldn't help it. She would love for the center to remain open and grow to open buildings in other communities, but at the moment, she couldn't see herself doing it.

Lord, make a way, Hannah prayed before entering the main meeting space of the center. She had remained in her office longer than she'd liked, making some calls and checking into people volunteering their time and services for a few of the larger events she had planned.

One change she had made right away was being sure to watch the volunteers more closely. Her dad had even blessed them and installed another camera near her office where she conducted a lot of the financial business for the center. Since the start of the week, Tamela seemed a little agitated, asking Hannah if she trusted her. She explained to her, April, and Ms. Reid that she needed to be more cautious after the money incident. Ms. Reid and April said they understood. Tamela didn't respond and walked away, which Hannah thought was odd.

A little more relaxed, satisfied with the changes she'd made so far, but still concerned about the state of the center, Hannah stepped to the front of the room ready to start tonight's Bible study. April stood off to the side smiling as she glanced around the room. Hannah was grateful April and Tamela had set up everything, so Hannah could take a few minutes to herself. Several women had shown up. They all gathered in a circle around the round tables as Hannah instructed and opened with prayer. Her emotions got the best of her as she began, "Lord, please provide for So That You May Live like never before and for the women here and those connected to it."

"Yes, Lord," a few of the women chimed in.

"Father, we thank You for what You have already done here. Help each of us to walk by faith and not by sight," Hannah cried. Unable to continue as her tears flowed, Ms. Joan took over, squeezing Hannah's hand, which made her feel stronger.

"Lord, we love and adore You. You are mighty in all Your ways. Give us the strength to climb over every mountain placed before us. Allow this Word tonight to soothe our hearts and calm our fears. We give You glory in advance, in Jesus' name. Amen."

"Amen," the women said in unison.

When they released hands, Hannah's tears were still flowing. The ladies had no clue with what she was dealing with. *Lord, these women need a place to grow and build their skills. Please make a way.* Ms. Joan held her for several seconds before she nodded and thanked the woman for her encouragement. Hannah felt the Lord's presence in the room. As the women began taking their seats, Hannah felt their love.

"All right, ladies. Are you ready to get started with the reading of God's Word?" Hannah asked.

A few of them said, "Yes, ma'am."

"Well, let's get into it. We are going to keep things simple this evening. Let's start with each of us sharing how things have been going for us and how we're feeling at the moment."

"Sounds good," said Isis, one of the members of Hannah's church.

"Well, I'll begin. As you all can probably tell, something has been weighing on me," Hannah explained, not wanting to tell any specifics. She wasn't sure how they would respond, so she kept her explanation vague. "Things were going really well, then something I would have never expected happened. I have been down about it, but I feel more encouraged after talking with my family members and being here with you all this evening. Anyone else want to share?"

"I'll share," Isis said. "Well, since I've been coming to your workshops and other events here, I've been feeling more inspired. I especially loved the Creative Purpose event. You should do that one again."

"That's awesome to hear. I'm so glad to hear you are enjoying hanging out with us here. I think I will host another one soon. You aren't the first one to mention it to me."

"Good. I can't wait," Isis said.

"Now, I thought that we could spend some time tonight walking through scriptures that assure us of God's love for us. Go with me to Psalm 147:3." Hannah waited a moment for the women to get there.

"It reads, *'He heals the brokenhearted and binds up their wounds.'* This scripture tells us that God cares about our broken hearts. He is ready and willing to heal us. How does that make you feel?"

"It makes me feel better," said Simone, one of the younger women from House of Hope Women's Shelter.

"Tell us what you mean by that," Hannah said.

"I have walked around for years thinking God doesn't care about me or what happens to me, but now I know that's not true," Simone said.

"Simone, would you believe I once felt the same way? But those who knew God around me helped me come to know him, and I now know he loves me."

"Wow. I can't see you thinking that way. Your faith seems strong."

"That's encouraging, especially after what I've been experiencing recently. I do believe more than I ever have, but it's still a day-by-day process for me as well," Hannah said. "Does anyone else want to tell us how this scripture makes you feel?"

"Can I share?" asked April, now sitting at one of the tables next to Simone.

"Yes. Please do," Hannah said.

"It lets me know that God wants to have a relationship with me because I have to allow him to bind up my wounds. It's kind of like if I got hurt and had a physical wound. I would have to go to the hospital to allow the medical professionals to tend to it, give me meds for it, and to wrap it up. They would also give me instructions on how long it would take to heal. It's the same with God. We have to come to him and allow him to give us instructions on how we can heal spiritually, then we have to allow him to do the work in our lives. We also have to trust that he has the cure to all our spiritual needs."

"Oh, that was good, sis," Hannah said. "I need to write that down."

"Me too," Simone added.

Hannah noticed the rest of the women remained quiet, nodding as they shared. She guessed they were just taking it all in. Many of them had shared that they hadn't really read the Bible.

"Alright. Now let's look at another psalm. Go to Psalm 63. Let's read verses 1 through 3 together." The women joined in as Hannah read, *"O God, you are my God; earnestly I seek you; my soul thirsts for you; my flesh faints for you, as in a dry and weary land where there is no water. So, I have looked upon you in the sanctuary, beholding your power and glory. Because your steadfast love is better than life, my lips will praise you."*

"Huh?" Amara said. "I don't really get that one."

"Well, let's break it down a little at a time. In the first part, King David is acknowledging his belief in God and that God is the God he serves."

"I kinda get that part," Simone said, "but why does he have to tell God that?"

"Well, the psalms are much like songs we sing, so picture King David looking up and talking or singing this to God—lifting up his voice, honoring God."

"Kind of like someone singing a worship song or even praying to God," April added.

"Oh, okay," Simone said.

"In these verses, King David is also telling God that he is seriously seeking after Him. The soul-thirsting and flesh-fainting parts show that there is a strong desire for God. He feels he can't make it without Him. Now, close your eyes for a moment. Can you imagine your soul thirsting or your flesh fainting?" Hannah asked.

The women were quiet for a moment, then Isis spoke. "Yes. I feel that way now. So, I think the scripture is telling me that I can't make it in this world without God."

"None of us can," Hannah said. "I know it seems that we can figure it all out on our own, but I have never experienced such love, despite what I'm going through right now. If I didn't know God, it would have knocked me back into depression."

"I also have felt like I was fainting in a desert, but things are getting a little easier. I don't want to go back to that feeling. I want to keep drawing closer to God's love, learning more, and letting him help me through my life's problems," Simone said.

"That's what he wants," Hannah said.

After discussing the next scripture, Hannah told the women she wanted them to take ten minutes to journal about their favorite one. They could write about whatever came to mind as it related to God and the scripture they chose. All the women began writing on the paper April had placed on the tables. Even Tamela and April were engaged in whatever they were writing.

As Hannah looked around the room, she was overjoyed at what God was doing tonight. Once the women finished writing, a few of them shared. Several said they preferred not to, so Hannah asked for any prayer requests, wrote them down on the notepad before her and began to pray specifically for the women God had entrusted her with. She prayed for their protection. She prayed for direction. She prayed for them to continue to seek Him. She prayed for their success in Him. She prayed for God's direction when the truth came to light. She still wasn't sure who had stolen the money, but she just wanted it back to help with this much-needed ministry. Finally, she prayed for the thief's repentance and restoration.

CHAPTER EIGHTEEN

Sunday, April 5

The following Saturday, Hannah was grateful for a celebration to take her mind off of the theft. She hadn't heard a final word from PayPal, so Officer Swift, the officer she'd filed a police report with, couldn't move forward with his investigation until then. Hannah wanted to know the outcome, but she could wait a little longer. She didn't want a gloomy cloud hanging over this very special day anyway. Today would be a full day for her and Levi. She was elated to be celebrating Ariel's fourth birthday.

Now that the church service was over, they were preparing to head home for the big shebang. Ariel hadn't stopped talking about it all week. She wanted all of their family there. Her daughter's birthday wasn't until Thursday, but they couldn't host her party then, and Hannah was swamped at the center on yesterday, so today was it. Hannah stood in line to retrieve Ariel from children's church.

Her aunt had also been on her mind more lately. Her mom wasn't in church today because she had remained with Aunt Loretta. She had told Hannah her aunt had been down since she'd talked her into filing a restraining order.

Lord, be with her and guide her, Hannah prayed.

She'd enjoyed service today. Of course, the Word was on time. "God is calling us to be soldiers and not wimps," Pastor Richardson had said.

Hannah laughed to herself as she reflected on his demonstration of the two. She knew it would take much strength to keep moving forward with the center. She knew she could do it because she was now a soldier for Christ. This entrepreneur journey was surely not for the weak.

As she neared the head of the line, she spotted Tamela coming out of the restroom and waved her over. Tamela seemed to hesitate. Hannah wondered if she was still frustrated with her for monitoring the volunteers more at the center, although she didn't know why she was so bothered with it. Yes, they were friends, but Hannah was doing what was best. She was trying to be a good steward over what God had placed in her hands, and she still wasn't sure who had stolen the donation money.

"Hey, sis," Hannah said, embracing Tamela.

"Hey. Don't you look beautiful in your hunter green. You are rocking that suit. And those coils are coiling," Tamela said, pretending to shout.

"*Awww*. Thank you. You look beautiful as well," Hannah said, wondering why her friend seemed to be trying so hard to sound enthused, but she was glad she was more upbeat at least.

"Thanks. That was a good word today, wasn't it?" Tamela asked.

"Yes, it was. Our pastor does not beat around the bush. All we can do is say, 'Ouch, Holy Spirit.'"

Hannah and Tamela shared a laugh. "That is so true," Tamela said.

"Well, I'm not going to hold you up. Tell Benard I said hello."

"I will. He is working again today, so he couldn't make it this morning."

"Oh, I hope he gets some time off soon. I know he misses church. Tell him we miss seeing him." "Okay, see you in a few, but I won't be able to stay long. I do want to drop off Ariel's gift."

"Okay, no problem," Hannah said before her friend walked away.

After signing Ariel out, Hannah headed back into the sanctuary to get Levi. He was inside still talking to a few of the men he'd connected with during their men's ministry meetups. They both loved their church. It was as if Pastor Richardson had thought about every area. No one was left out. They always had something for one age group or another.

"I'm ready to go start my party, Mommy," Ariel said, looking up at Hannah in her pink-flowered lace dress with her matching tiara and ribbons around her two curly afro puffs. Hannah thought she looked more like Levi. She was such a beauty. Their baby was growing up. She needed her to slow down a bit.

"We are going in a few minutes. Your party doesn't start until four. We're waiting on Daddy."

"Why is he taking so long?"

"Ariel, we just walked in here. Give Daddy a minute."

"Mommy, do you have a snack for me in your purse?" Ariel asked.

"I have some graham crackers," said Hannah reaching into her purse and handing Ariel the miniature size bag.

Hannah then eyed Levi, trying to let him know they were ready. He got the signal and hurried to end his conversation. He fists bumped his new friends and headed in their direction.

"Daddy, you were taking forever. I'm ready for my party," Ariel said, swinging her hips from side to side, dancing to imaginary music.

"Okay, Busy Bee. We're going now. You're excited."

"Yes. I'm almost at the number to start school," Ariel explained, pulling Levi's arm, trying to get him to walk faster.

"Is she trying to rush me?" Levi asked, leaning over to kiss Hannah.

"That's what it looks like," Hannah said.

"She gets this bossy spirit from you."

"Uh, no she does not," Hannah said, cracking up laughing now.

"Mommy, do you have more crackers?"

"Ariel, can you wait a bit until we get home?"

"No, Mommy. My tummy is still empty. I have to eat a little more before the party."

"Oh, Lord," Levi said. "You will live, busy bee."

"Are you sure?" Ariel asked, tracing circles on her belly and laughing. "Just kidding, Daddy."

Hannah looked at her husband and shook her head. "That's your child," he whispered as he walked to the driver's side to unlock the doors. They all climbed inside, and Hannah handed Ariel another small bag of graham crackers. *She didn't really eat much of her breakfast*, Hannah thought to herself.

***

Everyone had arrived, and the kids had been out back for more than an hour jumping in the bouncy house Hannah and Levi had rented, playing musical chairs with Levi directing, and having their faces painted by Aunt Brittany. There were only a few kids there—five of them whom Ariel had met at daycare. April's daughter, Jaya, was also there, and Hannah's niece, Neveah. Ariel was having the time of her life. She had screamed when Neveah and Brittany first arrived. Hannah loved the bond they had as cousins. She thought she was the oldest, instead of Neveah, so Hannah had to talk to her about not being so bossy as she tried to rush Neveah out of the bouncy house to make friendship bracelets.

Hannah and her mom had a long talk, and she had asked Hannah if her aunt could attend Ariel's party. Hannah had let her guard down enough to agree. When her aunt had arrived, she had sat in silence.

Mama Jefferson had taken her in Hannah and Levi's room to pray with her. Her aunt seemed to be in better spirits after that. She was sitting outside enjoying watching Neveah and Ariel play together. Hannah stood off to the side as she watched her aunt smiling when Ariel called her TT and asked her to come over and get her face painted. It warmed Hannah's heart.

She peeked through the patio door and said, "Ariel, you all will be eating in a few minutes. Then, we will get to the birthday cake," Hannah said from the patio door.

"Okay, Mommy," Ariel yelled as she watched Brittany paint Aunt Loretta's face.

"She is getting so big," Uncle Joseph said after Hannah returned to her seat in the living room.

"Yes, she is," Mama Jefferson said.

"I need her to slow down. She is almost in school," Hannah said. "I'm not ready."

"Well, you might as well get ready because it's coming," Hannah's mom said, giggling.

"It seems like you just had her," Aunt Melissa said.

"Don't remind me."

"Have you thought about what school you would like her to go to?" her dad asked.

"That's a year from now."

"Yeah, but it's not too soon to start checking them out."

"I guess. I haven't really had time to really think about it."

"Well, God will lead you to the right one," Mama Jefferson said. "I've been teaching her the letters of the alphabet when she's with me. With you and Levi working on numbers and colors, she's going to be more than ready."

"Ariel is a smart girl anyway. She picks up on things really fast," Hannah's mom said.

After chatting for a few more minutes, Hannah, her mom, and Mama Jefferson went into the kitchen to prepare the children's plates while her dad and uncle set up an extra folding table so everyone could eat inside because the flies were ruthless. A few minutes later, they called everyone inside to partake of the food.

After they had all eaten, Hannah called everyone into the dining room to sing happy birthday.

Publix bakery had done an amazing job with Ariel's cake. It was just how she wanted it. There was a young African American ballerina on the left side of the cake standing on her toes. She wore a pink tutu and ballerina shoes. The right side read *Happy Birthday, Busy Bee! Love, Mommy and Daddy!* Hannah nearly cried as she lit the candles.

As her family sang to their daughter, Ariel grinned and looked around. When they were done, she yelled, "Thank you! I'm a big girl now," as she held up four fingers.

"Yes, you are," Aunt Loretta said, walking over and giving Ariel a high five. She then looked up at Hannah and Levi and whispered, "Protect her."

"Oh, that's a given," Levi said. "I don't want to have to lose my freedom, but I will for this one."

"Oh, nobody's losing their freedom," Mama Jefferson said. "Ariel is covered under the blood of Jesus. The devil better get somewhere and sit all the way down."

"I know that's right," Hannah's mom echoed. "And the same goes for my other grand, Neveah."

"And these two are the Lord's gangsters," Levi said, kissing Mama Jefferson and Hannah's mom on the cheek.

That caused laughter throughout the dining room. Hannah needed this. After cake, they laughed and talked for hours, and she and Aunt Loretta talked a little bit more.

Keep working, Lord, Hannah thought. *Keep mending our relationship.*

CHAPTER NINETEEN

Friday, April 10

By the following Friday, Hannah was exhausted once again. April and Tamela had only been able to help out two days this week, her mother-in-law was helping prepare meals for those in need, and Ms. Reid still only held the counseling sessions. She assumed Tamela had something she needed to tend to, but Hannah hadn't talked to her friend much lately.

She was thankful that they were still getting in donations, some a little larger than others, and she had been on top of it. Her two-step verification was still in place. She had checked it several times, but she needed to know the truth about the theft.

She had only met with a few women today, so she was able to finalize the plans for the first bake-off. Hannah hoped it would bring in some more bigger donations and more women. Before heading home, she decided to check her email again for any communication from PayPal.

"Finally," she said, sighing.

As she read through their resolution, she found out that the money would not be returned because the IP address used was Hannah's business laptop, and the money appeared to be sent to the name listed several times, over several weeks. They told her she could take the resolution to the police department, and they would fully cooperate with them as they tracked down the person with the bank account and who they were connected to, but it still appeared that

Hannah sent the money to the individual. Hannah couldn't believe what she was reading. That meant someone in the center with her did steal the money—and from her laptop. The worst part was she would not likely have it returned to her business, and she didn't know who to trust at this point. Her head thumped at this news, so she packed up and prepared to leave.

As she locked up the center and headed to her car, Hannah prayed for strength to endure. She would get that information to Officer Swift as soon as possible. Tears welled in her eyes at the thought of it all. *Why would someone do this? I've poured my life into this center in just a few months.*

Hannah hoped her husband would be okay with some fast food because she just wanted to climb in the bed. On her way home, after picking up Ariel from daycare, Hannah found herself fighting off sleep as she drove.

She picked up KFC for them to have for dinner. Although they had gone grocery shopping just the other day and their refrigerator was packed with food, Hannah needed to eat something already prepared. She prayed Ariel was worn out because she needed her to sleep as well. As she headed home only a few blocks away, she tried to shake off sleep and the tears that kept on coming.

Once inside, Hannah groaned at the sight of their messy house. The living room was overdue for vacuuming and dusting. She looked up the hall at the two laundry baskets she'd washed on Saturday still sitting in the laundry room. Some of the clothes had been left thrown across the top of the dryer from their search for specific items for them or Ariel to wear. After instructing Ariel to go put her things into her room, Hannah turned the corner and walked into the kitchen. Shaking her head, she couldn't believe she'd forgotten about the dishes from breakfast this morning. They were piled high in the sink. They had a dishwasher, but Hannah and Levi never used it. They just took turns doing them. Tonight, Hannah didn't have the strength to do anything. They would have to wait unless Levi did them when he got in.

Hannah started some low instrumental gospel music through their Bluetooth speaker. Her heart was heavy with the news she'd just received, so she hoped the music would relax her a little. She then headed up the hall to their bedroom to slip out of her clothes and change into a pair of joggers and a t-shirt. She thought about how much she loved running the center and seeing the women grow. They'd had such fun with one another. Her mind was drawn back to Ms. Joan's song. She had to admit that she was one of her favorites. Hannah never pictured serving someone so much older than her.

God then brought Ms. Nettie to her spirit. Ms. Nettie was an older woman who lived at the shelter a few years back when Hannah would host workshops there. *Yes, Lord. I loved Ms. Nettie too. I'm so glad she is no longer at the shelter. I wonder if she is still living with her cousin in Tennessee.* Hannah hadn't heard from Ms. Nettie in some time. She prayed things were going well for her and the other women who once found shelter at House of Hope.

Hannah cried even more as she put away the folded clothes on their bed. She soon heard Levi come in, then walked into the master bathroom to dry her eyes.

"Babe, Ariel, I'm home."

"Daddy," Ariel yelled from a few steps away. Hannah could hear her little feet running up the wooden floors in the hallway.

"There's my little busy bee," Levi said.

Hannah drug herself out of their room and up the hallway, back into the kitchen where her husband stood, looking into the bags on the stove. He turned to look at Hannah, "Babe, what's wrong?"

"I finally heard from PayPal. I found out the thief is someone at the center. The report said it was over several weeks. I couldn't pull together any more strength to cook, so I picked up something."

"Babe, I'm so sorry to hear this," her husband said, walking over and wrapping his arms around her. "And all you want to do is serve those women."

"I don't know if I can do this anymore, Levi. This is too much. Maybe I'll just go back into the classroom and close down the center. I can find a different school or do some educational consulting work. This is too much. But then my other thought is to do what I can to keep serving and loving on those women. I'm reminded of the amazing times I've had with the women and seeing them change and us building one another up and being encouraged through God's Word. I feel I'm in my element when I'm helping them."

"Babe, I don't like how you are looking. This is taking a toll on you."

Hannah gave him a half smile. Ariel sat in her chair at their breakfast nook in the corner. She then said, "Mommy, Daddy, I'm hungry. Can we eat? I want some chicken and mash 'tatoes."

"Potatoes," Levi said, correcting Ariel. Then, Ariel put her arm to her mouth and pretended to chew on it. Levi eyed Hannah. "And then we have Miss Do the Most over here."

Hannah couldn't hold her laughter. "Leave my baby alone. She gets it from her daddy. She is a clown like you."

"*Ummm,* that would be a no," Levi said, cracking up. Hannah stood to grab paper plates from the pantry, but Levi held up his hand. "Babe, you sit down. I'll grab our plates. What do you want on yours?"

"A few mashed potatoes, a leg, and a thigh," Hannah said, "then, I'm going to bed."

"And I want 'tatoes and chicken," Ariel repeated.

"I heard you, Busy Bee," Levi said.

"Hurry up, Daddy. My tummy is about to fall out," Ariel said.

"Girl, your stomach is not going to fall out," Levi said, laughing uncontrollably this time. "That's your child."

"Nope." Hannah said, grateful for that moment of laughter. "She is even greedy like Daddy for sure."

"Oh, that's a low blow," her husband stated, grabbing at his heart.

"You are so dramatic, but really thanks for everything. I really mean it," Hannah said, tearing up again as her husband sat beside her. "I don't know what I would do without my tribe. I just want to run away from this mess at the center."

"First of all, you never have to thank me for anything," Levi replied, grabbing her right hand and kissing her knuckle. "Let's trust God on this one as we have before."

"I just want it to be over so I can move forward."

"It will be soon. Watch and see. Meanwhile, you are going to keep serving those women, and we are going to set a plan to support each other more at home. How about we make a few meals the next two weekends and purchase some meal prep containers? That way we continue being frugal with our money, and all we have to do is take our meals from the freezer and warm them up. Would that help?"

"That would be wonderful," Hannah replied.

"And I know I leave early in the morning, and we both get in late, but let's do our best to divide the chores more."

"I'll try to stick it out," Hannah said, her thoughts drifting back to the stress she'd had to endure in such a short time.

"Give it all to God, babe. Stop worrying."

"Thanks for all of the encouragement over the past few months," Hannah said, leaning in to kiss her husband.

"*Ewww,* Mommy and Daddy. Stop it, and eat your food."

"Really?" Levi said, scrunching his nose at Ariel. "You are not our boss, Busy Bee. We are your bosses."

Ariel giggled as she continued eating. Chicken grease covered her cheeks. "Daddy, a boy at daycare tried to give me a kiss."

"What li'l boy has lost his mind?" Levi asked, his eyebrows lifted.

"Oh, Lord," Hannah said, shaking her head.

"No, I will hurt one of those li'l boys at that daycare and be ready for their daddy," Levi said.

"You can't hurt people's children, sir, and no, we are not fighting daddies either," Hannah instructed, doubled over in laughter.

"Babe, I promise y—"

"Daddy, he didn't give me a kiss because I pushed him like that," Ariel said, demonstrating for Hannah and Levi, thrusting both of her hands forward in a pushing motion.

"That's what I'm talking about. That's Daddy's busy bee," Levi encouraged.

"No, Ariel. No hitting or pushing. I want you to tell your teacher if he does that again," Hannah said.

"Now why did you tell her that?" Levi whispered. "Tell those li'l boys they don't know her daddy. I don't play about my baby girl." He laughed, but Hannah knew he was as serious as a lung transplant.

"Let's finish eating and go to bed," Hannah said, sleep creeping in again.

"Sure, babe. Go ahead and finish up so you can go get some rest. I'll stay up and do the dishes and do some more cleaning and can put Busy Bee down."

"How did I get so blessed?" Hannah asked as she gobbled down her food.

"I am blessed to have such an amazing, beautiful wife and daughter," Levi said.

"Awww," Hannah said, blowing air kisses at Levi.

Hannah hung out with her husband and daughter for a few more minutes as she finished her food.

She then stood and headed to the shower. Once she'd finished and was in her Old Navy pajama shorts and top, she kneeled and prayed for the strength to keep going. She then climbed in bed and was fast asleep by the time her head hit the pillow.

CHAPTER TWENTY

Saturday, April 25

Hannah had yet to find out the details of Officer Swift's investigation, but she continued to remain vigilant as she went about the daily operations at the center. The bake-off had finally arrived, and the outside of the center was bustling with activity. This was her first community event, and Hannah prayed it would be a huge success. Many of her church members had helped her share on social media, and they'd put up flyers all around town and inside a few businesses who allowed it. She also got a few teens from her church, Giver of Life Ministries, to come out and assist with setting up the long tables they'd borrowed from her and Pastor Dickerson's church. Hannah wondered how she could get so many to help with today's event, but none had more time to assist with the center operations. She guessed most people worked, and those who didn't had other obligations, so she was grateful for what she could get today. Simone had also come over to assist her and April, her only center volunteer for today, with setup. Tamela couldn't make it for some reason. Her friend had been a little more distant lately. Hannah wasn't sure why.

Hannah, Simone, and April went around covering the tables with plastic lavender tablecloths, fresh flowers, and balloons. They also added balloons and streamers around the center door and front window. Hannah was ecstatic.

Even though she was still working around the clock for the most part, she'd been able to get a little bit more rest over the past few days. Her husband was at work but would be out later, and Ariel was coming with her mom, but Levi still continued to be an amazing support as to her as promised, and she didn't take it for granted. After decorating outside, Hannah and April went back inside. Hannah instructed April to finish preparing the price sheets and list of ingredients to tape on the table next to the desserts. They would print them out using Hannah's printer she'd brought in from home. While April worked, Hannah checked their business pages for any preorders online. Finding ten orders placed, she danced in her seat and made a list of the names, what they'd ordered, and how much. She knew it wasn't a huge list, but once again, it was manna from heaven. She didn't want to just replenish what was stolen; she prayed it would be above and beyond.

Hannah hurried because they only had an hour before the event began. The participants were instructed to be there at least an hour early. As she worked, her phone rang.

"Hello."

"Hey, sweetheart. Did you say there is a Zaxby's on the corner as you turn into the plaza?"

Aunt Melissa asked.

"Yes. Are you here?" Hannah asked, leaping from her seat. "Did you turn left on Century Road?"

"Yes. Do I turn in here at the Zaxby's?"

"Yeah. That's it. I'm coming out to meet you. Come down all the way to the end where you see the parking lot on the end with the tables and purple balloons outside."

"Okay. See you in a minute."

Hannah hurried and wrote down the last online order and headed outside. Her heart leaped when she saw Aunt Melissa and Uncle Joseph, and her dad was with them.

"Daddy?" Hannah mouthed. *He told me he couldn't make it because of work.* She jogged over to the car as they parked and began to unload. "I thought you were working today." She wrapped her arms around her dad in a bear hug.

"It wouldn't have been a surprise if I would have told you," her dad replied.

"How is my niece doing?" Uncle Joseph asked, walking up with Aunt Melissa.

"I'm doing pretty good now that I've gotten to see you all. I've missed you so much," Hannah said, hugging her aunt and uncle.

"What do you need help with?" Hannah asked, looking at her watch. "We have to start setting up."

"I love how my daughter is boss. Look at you, jumping right into your role."

"Oh, Daddy. Thanks for being here," Hannah said, wrapping her arms around her dad again. "You don't know how much your presence has encouraged me." Her dad and uncle unloaded the car, and Hannah led her aunt inside to take a seat.

Moments later, the other participants began to arrive—Hannah's mom, her sister, a few mothers from Pastor Dickerson's church, women from Hannah's church, and Mama Jefferson. By the time they were all unloaded, there was a sea of desserts all around them on the tables. Hannah instructed Ariel to stay with TT Brittany while she finished inside. April and Simone hurried to tape down the price and ingredients lists while Hannah went to check for more online orders. Her cell phone rang again.

Oh, I am tired of this phone. I have to get back out there.

So That You May Live

"Hello."

"Mrs. Jefferson, this is Officer Swift. How are you?"

Hannah's heart began to pound. *Finally.* "Uh, how are you? Have you found out anything about the name attached to the account?" she asked.

"I have. The bank account in the name of Cassandra Lee was traced to a Tamela Love."

"What? How?"

"She talked one of her cousins into letting her use her PayPal and savings accounts. I just spoke to the young lady. She told me everything, but she was confused at first. Tamela told her she would give her a portion of the money, and it was legit. Something about you paying her back a personal loan you owed her for helping you with the launching of the center, but she didn't want her husband to find out because he didn't know she had loaned it."

"That is a lie," Hannah said. "This woman is supposed to be my friend, and she's stealing from me, and she blamed my aunt. Why would she do this? Will she be arrested?" Hannah asked.

"No, because it doesn't prove that she stole the money. It still appears you sent each payment. It would be a case of your word against hers."

"I can't believe this. She had to have gotten my information from my phone one day when she was helping me. I don't know how she didn't think she would get caught."

"Well, Mrs. Jefferson, she may have thought you would never figure out about the deleted PayPal information."

"I don't know what else to say, but thank you for giving me a call."

"Not a problem," he said before hanging up. "Good luck with everything. I would advise not being logged into your accounts when you are not right there. Monitor them carefully, and whatever you do, don't give anyone the benefit of the doubt. You'd be surprised at what I've seen. Some people are just looking for an opportunity."

And I should have been more careful. "Thanks again, Officer Swift."

After hanging up, Hannah fumed. *How could she? She pretended to be a woman of faith and my close friend. Why would she do this? I've been nothing but kind to her. I was too trusting. That's why she stayed so close to me. So fake. I can't deal with this right now,"* she said, fighting back angry tears.

Gathering herself, Hannah then took a deep breath before walking back into the main meeting space where Aunt Melissa was sitting. She pasted on a smile and headed back outside to see if there was anything else needing to be done. Everything looked great.

A few minutes later, a group of buyers showed up as Hannah was speaking through the microphone and welcoming the participants and explaining to the buyers that they were giving to a worthy cause. She explained the vision of the center and shared how much of an impact they had already made and how much they could really use the donations from this fundraiser. Then, she instructed the growing crowd to enjoy and to purchase lots of tasty desserts. If they wanted to participate in winning a twenty-five-dollar gift card, they could cast their votes for the best baked goods ever in the jar on the small round table up front.

"You can also enter to win a free baked cake for your next holiday celebration," Hannah added.

Several *ooooh*s came from the crowd.

Trying to remain positive, Hannah headed over to check out her mom's table. She and her sister had decorated the table with a sunflower theme. "Mommy, can I help you?" Ariel asked.

"We are all done setting up. Can you help your Nana and TT sell their tasty desserts?"

"Sell them? I want to eat them," Ariel said.

"You can't eat them all," Brittany said.

"But I can try."

"No, ma'am," Hannah said. "I don't want all of your teeth falling out."

"No. I don't want that either."

They all laughed. Hannah told Ariel she had to walk around and talk to the people. She then hugged each of them and wished her mom luck. Her mom had baked pound, key lime, and red velvet cakes. Her mom had also made her famous banana pudding. Hannah then moved over to Mama Jefferson's table, drooling over the double chocolate and vanilla cakes she'd baked. Hannah was getting hungry watching the pieces being sliced and placed in containers as people purchased several slices. A few of the mothers had even prepared cupcakes, fresh baked cookies, cinnamon rolls, brownies lemon bars, coffee cakes, and pineapple upside down cakes. Hannah was overwhelmed, not knowing which one to try.

Next, she headed over to Aunt Melissa's table to see if she needed anything. "No. I'm okay. I'll let you know if I do."

Hannah walked the perimeter and chatted with the participants and those purchasing baked goods. She answered their questions, providing more information about the center and how they could sign up. Some wanted to help more, so she took them inside to complete sponsor forms. Hannah was becoming excited despite the news she had received about Tamela. God was providing more manna. She would raise more money.

As she returned, she continued greeting the guests and making new connections. Then, she noticed her Aunt Loretta coming across the parking lot carrying some containers, maybe to bring her mom something. She needed to let her aunt know what she'd just learned about Tamela. She felt awful even entertaining what Tamela had said about her aunt. *I really thought she was my friend.*

After dropping off the item at her mom's table, Aunt Loretta headed back across the parking lot. Hannah jogged to catch up to her.

"Auntie, how have you been?" Hannah asked, reaching her side and walking with her to her car.

"I'm doing okay. Everything looks great. I just love the work you are doing here."

"Thanks. I wanted to apologize for confronting you about the stolen donation money. I found out that it was Tamela."

"Oh, my God," her aunt said, shaking her head.

"Can we just put the past behind us, and can you come back and help me now that you have the restraining order against Malcolm? I'm going to have to let Tamela go."

"I would love to, Hannah. I'm so proud of you, my niece. I love and miss the times we spent together. I know you're not young anymore, but I would love to have that opportunity again."

"Me too, and I love you too, Auntie," Hannah said, stepping toward her aunt and hugging her.

When Hannah released her, Aunt Loretta said, "I can't wait to help with crisis counseling again and whatever else you need me to do."

"Oh, there is plenty. I want to put this behind me. The officer said it would be Tamela's word against mine."

"That's awful."

"Auntie, I thought she was my friend. Why would she steal from my center? Why would she pretend all that time?" Hannah asked, breaking down, tears flowing now. Aunt Loretta reached out to hug her, and she fell into her aunt's arms.

After a few seconds, Hannah stepped back from her aunt's embrace. She heard a car pull in next to where they stood. She turned to see the same black car. The driver got out, and her aunt's eyes grew wide.

"Malcolm."

Hannah just knew her eyes were playing tricks on her. She knew the devil himself was not in this parking lot.

"Auntie, let's go," Hannah said, pulling her arm, but her aunt wouldn't move. She just stared at her husband, trembling.

"Hey, baby?" he said, drawing closer to Aunt Loretta.

"Why don't you just leave me alone?"

"Auntie, come on."

"Shut up," Malcolm said, "and walk away."

"I have a restraining order. I know they served you at the house," said Aunt Loretta.

"I don't care about that. Where is my money?"

"Auntie, let's go," Hannah yelled.

"I said shut up and walk away."

"No. I'm not leaving her with you."

Her aunt stood in front of him sobbing. "Go away. What kind of man is not willing to take care of himself?"

"But how can I go away? I need money, and you're withholding it from me. I'm your husband," he said. "We've been married for twenty years. Some of those investments and retirement belong to me."

"You evil demon. You have lost every ounce of your mind showing up here. How did you find her?" Hannah asked, her anger rising, but she was also unnerved by his wicked smirk.

"I tracked that phone she has. She had no clue that I was following her. By the way, I know you and that piece of a mama of yours are behind her leaving me. You still feeding her those lies from all those years ago?"

"Wrong. It was all her choice, so I need you to leave," Hannah said, trying to maintain her composure. She wished she had her cell phone with her to call 911.

"Hannah, please let me handle this."

"Auntie, I'm not leaving you with this piece of a man."

"Hannah, please."

"No, Auntie. Let's go," Hannah continued, moving closer to her aunt.

Get help, Hannah heard in her spirit. Her heart pounded now. She didn't know what to do. He might take her aunt, and she didn't know what he would do. This man seemed desperate.

"Now, I need my money, and I might sign your little divorce papers."

"Daddy," Hannah screamed, spotting him at a nearby table checking out the desserts.

"Hannah, I can handle this," her aunt repeated.

"If you say one more word, I will kill Loretta right here," Malcolm said, lifting his arm, revealing a large hunting knife.

Hannah froze. *Lord, what do I do? Please protect her.*

"Hannah, go. I've got this," Aunt Loretta said in a low tone.

"What's going on?" her dad asked, closer now.

"Go away, Mal—" Aunt Loretta was saying before he stabbed her multiple times, and she crumbled to the ground.

Malcolm jumped in his car and sped off before her dad could reach him.

"Auntie. Auntie. He stabbed her," Hannah screamed as she and her dad kneeled beside Aunt Loretta. Her aunt's shirt was drenched in blood, and she held her chest. Hannah held her in her arms.

"Hannah…I'm sorry," her aunt struggled saying.

"Auntie, stay with me. I've got you."

"I love you, my sweet young lady," Aunt Loretta said.

"Auntie, hang in there. You've got to help me with the center."

As she held her aunt, she could hear her dad on the phone with 911 dispatch. An ambulance was on the way. Her dad then disappeared for a few minutes, and Hannah continued talking to her.

"Hannah, tell them to hurry," her aunt cried.

"They're coming, Auntie. Just keep talking to me."

"I'll try. I need help, Hannah."

"They're coming."

"Ok..ay."

Hannah felt led to ask her aunt a question, "Have you ever accepted Jesus Christ as your personal savior, Auntie."

"I ha…ve…not.."

"Would you like to?" Hannah sobbed, rocking back and forth, holding her aunt in her arms.

"Ye..s."

"Repeat after me."

"O..k..ay."

As Hannah said a shortened version of the sinner's prayer for her aunt, Aunt Loretta repeated the words. Her aunt cried as she said, "Com..e in.to my hea.rt I wa.nt to tr..ust you. I kn.ow I'm a sin..n..er. Sav..e me."

"He's doing it, Auntie."

"Te..ll tho..se la..dies I sa..id to li..ve," Aunt Loretta whispered through breaths.

"You are going to tell them because you will be here to help me."

"T..ell th..em fo..r me," Aunt Loretta continued. "Th..ey.. ha..ve to. Do..n't le..t no o..ne des..str..oy the..ir sp..ir..it..s. Tell th..em."

"Auntie, you are going to be fine. Stop talking. It's taking too much for you to talk. Just breathe. I'm praying fo..."

Just then, Hannah heard her mom's voice behind her, "No, no. Loretta," her mom screamed, kneeling beside Hannah.

Her aunt's breathing was growing more shallow as her dad and uncle helped pull her from Hannah's arms.

"Princess, come on. I've got you," her dad said, sounding far away.

"Daddy, is she going to be okay? I need her to be okay. Where is Ariel?"

"Brittany has her," her mom said, through tears.

Hannah couldn't tell if an hour or minutes had passed before she heard the wailing sound of the ambulance. She knew her dad was still there with her and others surrounded her and her mom, but she was in a daze. She could hear her dad telling her to let the paramedics take care of her aunt.

"Let's get you to the hospital with your mama."

"Okay," Hannah cried, her legs feeling like jelly.

"I'll call Levi," she heard Mama Jefferson say.

"We'll shut everything down for you," April said, standing beside her, holding her hand. "Don't you worry. Go see about your aunt. Where are your keys?"

"They're in the office. Can you bring me my bags?" Hannah asked April.

"I got you. I'll be right back."

"Mama?"

"I'm here," her mom said. Hannah ran into her arms.

"Mama, is Auntie going to be okay? She has to be okay. Please let her be okay," Hannah whaled. "Why did she marry that evil man?"

"I don't know," Hannah's mom said, still crying as they held each other.

Her dad led them both to Hannah's car. Hannah climbed in the backseat as her dad took the driver's seat and her mom the passenger seat.

Why did this happen, God? Why? Hannah prayed in her heart, laying her head back on her seat as she waited for her bags so they could make their way to the hospital behind the ambulance.

CHAPTER TWENTY-ONE

Saturday, April 25

Hannah sat in the Forest Park Piedmont intensive care unit waiting room with her head in her hands. Levi sat beside her, rubbing her back. Her dad, Uncle Joseph, and Aunt Melissa sat across from them. Her husband, Uncle Joseph, and Aunt Melissa had arrived about twenty minutes after they had. Mama Jefferson had taken Ariel, so Levi could be with Hannah. The doctors had told them they weren't sure if Aunt Loretta would regain consciousness. When she was stabbed in the chest, he severed a major artery, and her aunt was bleeding internally. That was not what Hannah wanted to hear. Why was this happening? She needed her to wake up.

Hannah's mom and sister were in the back seeing her aunt. Hannah was terrified. She wasn't ready to accept that she may not ever talk to Aunt Loretta again. No matter what she'd been through while living with her, she loved her aunt, and she needed to talk to her. They had so much in common. They both loved serving and helping others. Hannah could have just drug her aunt away from Malcolm. Hannah couldn't understand how someone could be so wicked. That man tried destroying her and other girls' innocence, and now he was destroying her aunt's life.

"How could he be so evil?" Hannah asked, looking at her husband. "I've never encountered a man like him. You, Daddy, and Uncle Joseph are amazing men."

"Babe, every man isn't, but there are more of us than him. Don't you forget that," Levi said with anger in his voice.

"He just drove away."

"Babe, I'm so glad you're okay," Levi said, wrapping his right arm around her tighter.

A few seconds later, Hannah's mom and sister returned to the waiting room for her and Levi to go in to see Aunt Loretta. Hannah couldn't take her eyes of their tear-streaked faces. Levi stood and attempted to grab her hand. Hannah snatched it away. She couldn't go.

"Come on, Hannah. You can do this," Aunt Melissa said, standing and reaching out to her.

"I can't. I don't want to see her like that."

"You've got this, baby girl," came her dad's soothing voice.

"You know she would want to hear your voice," her mom added.

Numb, Hannah sat there for a few more seconds before she stood. Levi wrapped his arms around her and took slow steps out of the waiting room. Once they entered her aunt's room, Hannah turned her face away for a moment. There were beeping machines all around her, and tubes ran all through her aunt's body. Levi grabbed a stool so she could sit next to the bed. She stood and stared in disbelief for several moments, then Hannah sat and grabbed her aunt's hand, caressing it.

"Auntie, please wake up for us. Please wake up. I love you so much," Hannah cried. "Our family is being restored. Please, Auntie. I know Mama has been enjoying you hanging out with her. I also saw a glow in your eyes when you were helping the women at So That You

May Live. I think you've found your purpose. I need you, Auntie. Now, we need you to live so you can continue in it."

"Aunt Loretta, we haven't really had a lot of conversation, but I believe you are a strong and amazing woman," Levi said. "You've gotta get up out of that bed and keep showing the world how great and brave you are. Your sister, nieces, and great nieces need you." He rubbed her arm.

A nurse entered the room with a clear bag of clothing and a purse. Hannah assumed they were her aunt's, "Oh, I thought her sister had come back in here. I wanted to give her the patient's clothes. I went to the waiting room but didn't see her."

"I'm her niece. My mom and sister might've gone down to the cafeteria to get something to eat," Hannah said.

"Well, I'll leave them with you," the nurse continued.

"Thanks," Hannah said through fresh tears.

"I'm sorry about your aunt, sweetie."

"Thanks again," Hannah said before the nurse exited the room.

Hannah lifted the bag because she noticed a note or something that must have fallen out her aunt's purse. There was some writing on it. Curious, she lay it on her lap and slid it out.

"What's that?" Levi asked.

"I don't know," Hannah said, unfolding the stained piece of paper. "It's a letter to Mama."

"Well, maybe you should wait and let her read it," Levi said.

Before she could put it down, she had scanned through the contents.

Tamika, Please don't be upset with me when you find this note. Thank you so much, sis, for being there for me during this time. Thank you for allowing me to live in your place to get away from that crazy husband I married. I have been so afraid of losing my freedom because I believe he is so low that he will lie to the police just to keep me married to him. I hate I had to leave my own house for all this time. I'm so sorry again for everything that happened with Hannah in the past.

Sis, I really don't know how to get out of this situation. He continues to threaten my life, and I've been terrified. He doesn't care about the restraining order. He said he's been tracking my every move. When Hannah mentioned someone in a black car, I started seeing a black car, like the one she described, when I would go to the grocery store or other places. I thought I was being paranoid. The car must be a rental. This is just becoming too much, so I think I'm going to find somewhere else to go, even if I have to stay in a hotel. I don't want him to try and do anything to you all. I never thought he would get this crazy. I've really enjoyed my time with you. It was the most fun I've had in a long time. I'm so sorry about this. I love you and will miss you, my dear sister.

"Oh, my God," Hannah gasped, covering her mouth.

"What?"

"She was planning to leave. He had been following her all around."

"That dude is messed up," Levi said. "We gotta make this guy pay for what he has done."

"We're going to try," Hannah said, continuing to read the letter.

I don't want to have to leave you all. It wasn't until I started helping Hannah at the center that I felt more encouraged and started trusting in God a little more. At one point, I didn't believe in God. Can you believe that, sis? Even though we had been raised up to have faith, I stopped believing, especially after the way Daddy rejected you and never spoke to you again. I was so angry. He's supposed to be a preacher. I wondered if that is what God was like too. I stopped communicating with Daddy as well. Not to mention, I couldn't have any children due to endometriosis. Then, when Mama died from cancer, I lost all faith in God.

For years, I lived on my own terms but didn't know I had married a deceiver and a liar. I should have left him before Hannah ever moved in with us because he couldn't keep a job. When you told me about Hannah's little miracle after her experience with endometriosis, I started thinking more about God, but I never felt a tug at my heart—until now.

I've been wrestling with my thoughts so much. I loved him with my whole heart, but he was doing the work of Satan. That's why I wanted so much to keep helping Hannah and those other women, and Malcolm even took that from me. I just felt I could help them not make the horrible choices I've made, but I can't take it anymore. Malcolm continues to threaten me because he doesn't know what I've done with my money. Yes, I've moved it—all of it—and I only told you where it is. Why should he have my hard-earned money? I've worked since I was sixteen. Why does he feel he deserves any of it? He still refuses to work. Anyway, I know I'm rambling, but I just wanted to let you know that leaving might be easier. I didn't have the courage to tell you in person.

Hannah sobbed into her aunt's bedsheets. She couldn't believe she might not pull through this, and that she felt she couldn't move past the evils of her husband, so running away was better for her, but she didn't even get the chance to do that.

"Why, Lord?" Hannah cried out.

"Babe, we are going to believe that everything will be okay," Levi said, leaning over to hug her.

"Levi, what makes women believe they can't get out of these situations with these dudes?"

She should have changed her phone number or something. We could have helped her more."

"I don't know, babe."

"Us younger women are supposed to learn from the older ones. If they feel they can't make it, what about us?"

"That's the importance of trusting in Christ. He didn't equip us to carry all of that weight alone. We have to give it to him. Aunt Loretta may have been dealing with a lot for years," Levi said.

"I hate that this happened," Hannah added.

"You ready to head home and come back tomorrow?" Levi asked.

"I don't want to leave her."

"I know, but we have to check on Ariel. You can come back tomorrow."

Hannah refolded the letter and stuffed it back into the bag that contained her aunt's other belongings.

She then paused, having a thought. *I will reach out to the saints to pray for Aunt Loretta, and I will hold an evening of prayer at the center. Satan doesn't win.* She grabbed her cell phone from her purse to text her pastor, Pastor Dickerson, and Pastor Gibson for them to send it out through their prayer chains and to announce the time of prayer that would take place at the center.

"Babe, you ready?"

"Yes," Hannah said, standing with a fight in her spirit.

She and her husband locked hands and headed back into the waiting room where the others had returned. She didn't see her dad, Uncle Joseph, and Aunt Melissa; only her mom and her sister remained.

"Did everyone else leave?" Levi asked.

"Yes. They said they had a long drive, so they would call you in the morning," Brittany said.

Hannah's mom seemed to be in a daze. Hannah walked over and sat next to her.

"Mama, did you try to eat anything?"

"No. I just want my sister to be okay. I tried getting word to that sorry father of ours through Cousin Verl."

"What did she say?" Hannah asked.

"She called him and got the message to him about Loretta. She told him to give me a call. I gave her my cell phone number. He hasn't called yet."

"Ah, Mama. Why are people like that?" Hannah asked.

"I don't know, and to think I was selfish and hateful like him once upon a time too."

"He may still call," Brittany said.

"I hope he does. That's his daughter laying in that bed in there," her mom added.

"Well, let's just try to go home and get some rest," Levi said.

"You all go ahead," Hannah's mom replied. "I'm going to stay here tonight in case there is some change."

"Mama, I don't want to leave you up here by yourself," Brittany said.

"Right," Hannah stated.

"I'm not by myself. I've got all these doctors and nurses walking around here, and most of all, I've got the Lord with me."

"We know that, Mama, but we don't want to leave you up here alone," Hannah said.

"Levi, take these two out of here so they can tend to my grandbabies. I will be fine."

"Alright then, Miss Sassy. I love you," Brittany said, leaning over to kiss their mom's forehead.

"I love you too."

"Love you, Mama," Hannah said, hugging her mom tight.

"I love you too, sweetheart. Now, get on out of here, and go get you some rest. You too, Brit. Don't you have to work tomorrow night?"

"I'm supposed to, but I don't know if I will. It depends on Aunt Loretta's condition."

"Oh, okay. Well, you still need some sleep. I'll call you all if something changes."

"Okay," they each said.

Just then, Hannah remembered the letter, reached into the bag, and handed it to her mom, along with everything else in it.

"What's this?" her mom asked.

"It's for you," Hannah said.

"Is it from you?" her mom asked, confusion on her face.

"No. It's from Auntie."

"Huh?" Hannah's mom said, more confusion on her face now.

"Just read it, Mama," Hannah finally said.

Before they left, Levi hugged and kissed Hannah's mom. Levi walked Hannah to her car and made sure she was safe inside. He then headed over to his car and followed behind Hannah. Her mind was still in a hazy fog on the drive home. One thing was for certain, she could not see herself continuing the center if her aunt didn't make it. That would be the turning back point for her. This was too unsettling, and the loss of her aunt would be unbearable. No, she wasn't equipped for this, and more of her strength was depleting every second her Aunt Loretta remained unconscious.

CHAPTER TWENTY-TWO

Friday, May 1

After another long week at the center, time at the hospital, and missing dinner with her husband and daughter, Hannah felt this evening of women praying together at the center was what she needed. The center had been slow all week because the incident with her aunt had spooked several of them. She prayed their fears would minimize over the coming days and they would return soon.

After the incident, Hannah was told the crowd thinned out and not many more showed up. A few more ongoing monetary donations had come in online, but that was all.

She hadn't seen nor heard from Tamela after attempting to contact her a few times. She was sure she'd talked to her cousin Cassandra by now, and that's why she was avoiding her. Thinking about how her so-called friend lied on her aunt, Hannah became angry again, but she knew her mind needed to focus on interceding for Aunt Loretta.

At that moment, Hannah didn't want to worry about how much help she had, about Tamela, nor about any money. No, Hannah wanted to focus on the fact that God could fix it all, and He continued to speak to her about the purpose of the center.

Ariel was with her mother-in-law, and Levi was working. She was relieved Ms. Priscilla would be in attendance tonight. She had agreed to pray.

Hannah parked and shuddered as she got out. She could still see herself holding her aunt in her arms.

She headed inside to set up some worship music and the microphone before the women began to arrive.

As she was unlocking the door, she turned to see Amara's car pulling in, then Ms. Joan's. Hannah smiled, glad to see them both. They got out and came over to hug her.

"Oh, Hannah. I'm so sorry about your aunt. She is a beautiful lady, inside and out," Ms. Joan said.

"Thank you, Ms. Joan. I'm so glad to see you both," Hannah said.

"We had to be here. Aunt Loretta has been a blessing to us," added Amara.

"Thank you, ladies, so much."

They headed inside, and the ladies helped Hannah with organizing the main meeting space a little. Soon, Pastor Dickerson and a few of the women from his church showed up. Hannah waved, excitement filling her heart. She was surprised to see him. She assumed it would only be the women who attended the center tonight.

"Hello. How are you?" Hannah asked, walking over to Pastor Dickerson, inviting him and the ladies to take a seat wherever. He gave her a hug. "I didn't know you would be here."

"God led me here to pray with you ladies."

"Pastor Gibson is on the way as well. She's picking up some water bottles."

"Really? I'm so thankful for the support."

"We are not just your board members. We are your brother and sister in Christ."

Hannah blinked back tears. When her pastor walked in, she nearly ran to hug him. She gave him a big hug, wiping away tears. "Pastor Richardson, you didn't tell me you were coming."

"I'm here to support you and your mother however I can. By the way, anymore word on your aunt?" Pastor Richardson asked.

"No change. Mama is up there with her now."

"Well, we are going to pray like we've never prayed before."

"Yes, we will," Hannah said.

As her pastor and Pastor Dickerson chatted, Hannah talked with Ms. Joan and Amara for a few minutes. She had come to enjoy these two women. She couldn't believe Ms. Joan had opened up so much. When she first came to the center, Hannah thought the woman would be too difficult to deal with. Now, she was the one who was blooming the most.

Soon Ms. Priscilla and a few more women arrived and joined them at their table. Minutes later, Hannah started. She asked everyone to quiet down and silence their cell phones. Next, she explained that they were there to intercede for her aunt and anyone else who was sick or dealing with something difficult. She explained that someone would come up and lead in prayer every few minutes, and everyone else could walk around the area, kneel, or stand still. It was up to them. She then asked her pastor to begin prayer, and Pastor Dickerson was to follow. Everyone stood all around the room as Pastor Richardson invited God's presence in and prayed for Aunt Loretta and that God's justice would prevail.

"Father, we know You are the God of Justice, so we ask that justice would come forth for the crime that was committed again Sister Loretta. I pray that Your will be done in her life. She is in Your hands, and we know those are the best hands any of us could be in.

God, we bless You, for You created Loretta, and we know You love her with an everlasting love."

As her pastor prayed, Hannah thought about how much more she wanted to help the women who would enter this space. She had to. There was no turning back. *Lord, give me the strength to press forward.*

Next, Pastor Dickerson prayed for Hannah's family's strength and for the women to return and continue to grow. Hannah was called up to the mic next to pray. She prayed for women dealing with some form of abuse. She prayed that women would know their worth. "Lord, help all of us to know You've made us for greatness. Let us never forget it. Help us to never again let someone reduce our value. Help us not to be afraid to walk away," Hannah said.

Ms. Joan and Amara came up and stood with her as she cried out for God's will to be done in her aunt's life.

Next, Ms. Priscilla came up and prayed for spiritual healing. "Dear Heavenly Father, I come to You this evening asking You to draw each of us closer with Your love. So many have experienced a warped view of love. Many here may have been hurt by someone close to them, so they view You through the lens of their pain. But Father, we know that You are good. You can heal every one of our broken places. You know the questions we have, and You know the purpose You have for our lives." As Ms. Priscilla prayed, several of the women lifted up their hands and cried out to God.

After an hour, women were still coming forward to pray for her aunt and their own situations. Hannah's heart was so full. She never envisioned this, but she appreciated how the Holy Spirit moved and hadn't let up yet.

CHAPTER TWENTY-THREE

Sunday, May 17

"Glory to God," various voices shouted across the sanctuary of Giver of Life Ministries.

"Come on, saints. Talk to me this morning," Hannah's pastor, Pastor Richardson, shouted back at the congregation.

Hannah inhaled and exhaled, trying to release the tension from her shoulders. It had been over three weeks since Aunt Loretta had been in the intensive care unit. She was now in a deep coma, and there was still no change in her condition. Hannah continued to pray, hoping her aunt would soon awake, no matter what the doctor's said. She was exhausted, but she tried to keep the faith.

Her pastor had spoken to her after the evening of prayer. She told him how she felt about not continuing with the center. She had made the payment on the leasing of the building for the next six months before the bake off, so she would finish out the year, then close down. Pastor Richardson had tried to encourage Hannah to keep going forward, but she had made up her mind. Things looked glim as it concerned her aunt, and she was done. She loved the ladies, but it was all just too much for her.

Since her aunt had been in the hospital, Amara and Ms. Joan had been her saving grace. They had come in to help keep the center running for her as much as possible, but since the theft, Hannah felt she had to be there to keep an eye on things. Then, she would stop by the hospital when she closed up. She trained Ms. Joan how to host some of the workshops because most of the time she remained in her office because she just didn't have the strength to assist with anything else.

She fought back tears as her pastor continued teaching from Matthew chapter 16. "Who do you say he is?"

"You are my Lord and savior," Hannah whispered, her head bowed, "and I need You to give me comfort right now."

Her husband pulled her into a hug. Her mom sat on her left, and she looked the way Hannah felt.

"As I close, I want you to remember that we must know who He is as Peter tells us in this scripture. When we know who He is, the gates of hell can't prevail against us."

"Preach, preacher," shouted Mr. Roosevelt, one of their members. He then stood and lifted his hand. "Say it, sir."

When we know who he is, we understand his power, and we understand his authority, church.

Therefore, don't lose hope. Hold to His unchanging hand. We don't hold our tomorrow in our hands, He does, and He knows the way."

"Yes, Lord," Mr. Roosevelt said, taking his seat.

"So, at this time, I'm calling those forth who feel you need prayer for anything."

Hannah loved that the Holy Spirit always knew what she and others needed when they needed it.

In times past, she wouldn't have stood to walk to the front of the church for prayer, but she had grown beyond that. And she and her aunt could use as much prayer as possible right now. She stood, grabbing her mom's hand to join her. Many followed as they made their way to the altar. As her pastor led them in worship through song first, Hannah poured her heart out to God for Aunt Loretta once again. She held her mom as she pleaded with the Lord for her sister's health. Pastor Richardson came down to pray with Hannah and her mom.

Hannah continued praying for women as a whole as she had been since witnessing what had happened to her aunt, *Lord, only you know what is best for Aunt Loretta. I pray for each woman you send to come to know Christ as Lord and Savior. Make provisions for them to make it outside of living in a shelter or hotel efficiency. God, send the husbands you have for those women who will be married, ones who will love them as you love each of us. We need you. Auntie needs you. Your will be done, in Jesus' name. Amen.*

After praying and covering Hannah and her mom, Pastor Richardson had begun praying specifically for her mom's deliverance and healing from her past. He told her that God wanted her to tell her story of overcoming like Hannah. Women elders surrounded them. They placed their hands on her mom's back.

"Thank You, Lord," one of the elders shouted.

"Do it, Lord," Hannah said. "Be with her and continue to lead her. Thank You for Your love."

Once Pastor Richardson finished, Hannah and her mom headed back to their seats. Levi put his arms around Hannah again, and she leaned over, laying her head on his shoulder while Pastor Richardson and the other leaders prayed for others at the altar.

After several more minutes, Pastor Richardson returned to the pulpit and thanked everyone for joining them in prayer for those who had come up. He then told them they had a few announcements.

The men's ministry leader went up first, then the announcements for the children's and teens ministry. Finally, Ms. Priscilla, her mentor, announced the next women's ministry meetup date and theme "Refreshing Grace." That sounded like something Hannah needed to attend, but at the moment, she only wanted to curl up in her bed and sleep so she didn't have to think about anything she was experiencing.

***

After leaving church, Hannah dropped Levi and Ariel off at home so he could get their daughter down for a nap. She and her mom were headed back to the hospital to check on Aunt Loretta. Her mom told Hannah and Levi that she would purchase them something to eat, so neither of them had to worry about cooking.

They headed back to Hannah's car and made their way to the hospital. She prayed there was some change. Her mom was pretty quiet as they drove. She only spoke when Hannah asked if she was hungry.

Both starving, they decided to stop at Jim 'N Nick's barbecue restaurant, which was near the hospital, to eat before heading over. Inside, Hannah noticed there weren't many people there. They were led to a small booth near the back.

"Mama, you feeling okay?" Hannah asked.

"A little. Just worried about Loretta."

"Me too. I pray she pulls through," Hannah said.

"I do too. I'm still shook about what happened to her, and he left her there. And I'm so glad he didn't harm you. Lord, have mercy."

"I don't even want to think about it," Hannah said. "I heard 'Go get help' in my spirit, but I was afraid to leave her, but it didn't matter. He didn't care."

"Can I get you ladies something to drink to start you off?" asked Missy, their very young-looking waitress. Hannah wondered if she was even old enough to be working with her pigtails on each side of her head.

"Yes. Can I get a strawberry lemonade?" Hannah asked.

"And can I have a sweet tea with lemon added?" her mom replied.

"Gotcha. I'll be right back with those drinks for you."

"Thanks," Hannah said. "Oh, and can we get some biscuits?"

"Yes. They are coming up. They had to bake some more."

"Thanks," Hannah said again.

"I need you to remain safe, you hear me?" her mom scolded as the waitress walked away.

"Yes, ma'am. Mama, my feet just wouldn't move."

"I just want you and those other women to stay safe. These jokers out here are crazy. I don't know why Malcolm feels my sister needs to take care of his grown tail. She should have left him before now, but I can't judge her. I've made some dumb decisions myself. I'm thankful for seeing the Jesus in you so I could come to know Him."

"Oh, wow. It's all Him, Mama. I pray that everyone can have a true encounter with Him. He is the truth," Hannah said.

"Yes, He is. If it weren't for Him, I would've returned to drinking over these past few weeks."

"I'm so glad you didn't. I have to admit I'm also struggling right now. I don't know how I will handle it if Auntie doesn't make it, Mama," Hannah said.

"You are going to be...as a matter-of-fact, we are going to be fine. You don't know how much I thank God for a second chance with you. I'm here for you no matter what."

"I know you are. I love you, Mama."

"I love you more. You keep trusting God."

"I pray He does," Hannah said. "By the way, did you read Auntie's letter?"

"I did. It broke my hea—"

"Here you are, ladies," Missy said, interrupting their conversation, dropping off their drinks.

"Oh, this is good," Hannah said, savoring every sip of her strawberry lemonade.

"They are good. That's all I drink," Missy added.

"Mama, you should try one."

"No. I'm good with the sweet tea."

"Are you ladies ready to order?"

"I am," Hannah said, having eaten there several times already. "I'll take the pulled pork, baked beans, and collards."

"Gotcha. And what about you, ma'am?" Missy asked, turning toward Hannah's mom.

"I would like the quarter chicken, mac and cheese, and collards as well."

"Alright, and here's your biscuits," Missy said after another waitress handed her a basket of fresh bread. "Your food should be up shortly."

"Okay. Thank you, sweetheart," Hannah's mom said. Once the waitress walked away, she continued, "Yes. That letter broke my heart. I didn't know she was planning to leave."

"And the restraining order she had on him didn't do any good," Hannah said.

"I know. The police wouldn't have gotten there in time."

"There's no telling where he is."

"Right. But I pray for mercy and salvation for him. He has mistreated the wife who stood by him for years as well as several girls."

"With no remorse," Hannah added.

"I'm going to fight to have him arrested if it's the last thing I do."

They chatted more while they waited for their food to come out. Hannah wasn't sure what was ahead, but she was grateful for that moment with her mom and for the opportunities God had already given her.

CHAPTER TWENTY-FOUR

Wednesday, June 13

After a month in intensive care with no change, Hannah's mom had made the decision to allow her aunt to go in peace. Aunt Loretta's funeral was the following week, and Hannah was devastated. All the praying for a turnaround, and that was the outcome. Her heart ached, and anger creeped in.

How could my aunt die? Lord, I don't get it.

Hannah's grandfather showed up with his other family. He cried as if he had been there for his daughters all these years, which made things tense.

The best part about the funeral was when her brother walked in late. Her sister, Brittany, was able to reach him after leaving several messages about Aunt Loretta. He was so handsome and looked dapper in his Marines uniform. He wasn't there long, but Hannah had the opportunity to speak with him. It was his mother's sister, so he was able to get permission to attend. Malik didn't have much to say to their mom, but he promised to return when he had another opportunity. Hannah told him not to let it be at another funeral.

He promised it wouldn't.

The other good thing was when her mom looked into her grandfather's eyes at the gravesite and spoke the simple but not so simple words, "I forgive you." He didn't respond, but that was when Hannah knew God had really changed her mother's heart. She admired her mother so much. Hannah needed to be able to forgive Malcolm for harming her as a child and for taking aunt's life, but she was struggling.

Since her aunt's passing, Hannah couldn't stand to be in the center. It reminded her too much of her aunt. Not that she did much on it, but the celebration of her birthday would never be the same. Hannah's birthday was this past Friday, but it had been overshadowed by her aunt's funeral. She was still numb, and she didn't know how she was expected to get women to believe and trust God when her aunt had been taken at fifty-six. Hannah had trusted God. She had believed her aunt would pull through but she hadn't. *Why did she have to die?*

The center had been closed for a few weeks as she grieved. Hannah still had enough grant money to last to the end of the year. Then, she would close, like she had already decided. She would reopen at some point, but at the moment, she just couldn't get past her aunt's untimely death. She informed the board that she needed more time. They understood. She had placed a *Closed Temporarily* sign on the door, sent out emails, messages, and hadn't been back.

As she sat at her kitchen table, she struggled to make sense of it all. Levi had left for work, and Ariel was at daycare, so she was alone with her thoughts. She hadn't done any Bible journaling in days. She didn't want to read any scriptures. Hannah didn't want to pray. She didn't want to talk to anyone—only her immediate family. When she reopened, she would only be open a few days a week for now, to reduce costs and preserve remaining funds and donations.

Right now, Hannah just wanted to run and hide from God's voice. He continued to tell her to move forward, but how could she?

Her cell phone rang, and she didn't recognize the number, so she didn't answer. The person left a voicemail. She listened to it. It was Ms. Joan. She called her back.

"Hey, Ms. Joan. How are you?" Hannah asked, trying to sound upbeat.

"How are you? I'm just checking on you."

"I'm doing okay."

"Would you be willing to hang out with me today? I was planning to go to the Atlanta Botanical Garden."

"*Ummm,* I really don't feel up to going anywhere, Ms. Joan."

"I want to help lift your spirits the way you have helped me so much at the center."

Taking a deep breath, Hannah didn't respond for several seconds. Then she said, *"Ummm."*

"Come on. Just for a little while this morning."

"Okay, I guess. I'll do it for you."

"Great! What's your address?" Ms. Joan asked.

Hannah recited her address and stood slowly, knowing she needed to get dressed. "I guess I'll see you soon," she said.

"Yes, ma'am. I'll be there in an hour."

"Okay," Hannah said.

***

Arriving at the Botanical Garden in the middle of the week seemed to be a great time. The crowd was small. As Hannah and Ms. Joan paid and began to take it all in, Hannah began to feel better. She had never been here before, and the place was breathtaking. Her heart leaped at the stunning array of colorful flowers, the gentle rustle of the leaves causing a cool breeze, the sound of the fountains of water, and the song of the birds. It all brought a great calm to her spirit.

I need to come here more often, Hannah thought.

As they walked through, enjoying every moment, Hannah and Ms. Joan had a heart to heart. Hannah had no idea that Ms. Joan was so caring. They found a bench in a back corner behind some large plants and continued their conversation.

"I'm so glad you're enjoying yourself. I figured you would."

"Thanks for getting me out of the house, Ms. Joan. I appreciate it."

"I really wanted you to do something for your birthday, and I can see the sadness in your eyes, dear."

"Really?" Hannah asked.

"Sure. Your eyes light up when you are helping us at the center. I know you love it. I don't see that light now. You are the reason I keep coming. You have a beautiful spirit."

"Oh, Ms. Joan. I'm not perfect at all. I just try to help women the way God used others to help me."

"I know you are not perfect. None of us are. You didn't know that I struggled with trusting others for many years. I have been hurt more than I'd like to admit. My husband passed several years ago, and I've only spent time in church and at home. I don't have many friends, and the women I felt I could trust from church, I was sadly mistaken. All they seemed to want to do is talk about what others were doing, so I just kept to myself."

"I've experienced something similar just recently," Hannah said, not wanting to mention Tamela to Ms. Joan.

"It can be a mess at times, but then I met you, your mom, your aunt, and some of the other women at the center. I saw your hearts for God and wanting to help others, and I wanted to keep being around you."

"Oh, wow. Thank you for sharing that, Ms. Joan, but I don't know if I will be able to continue with the center. It's just too much to handle. I'm not equipped to carry this kind of weight. My spirit is depleted. I don't have the desire to do it anymore."

"Dear, you have helped us more than you will ever know. I have let down my guard and shared more than I have in years. I've felt alone, even in the church at times, but not anymore."

"That shouldn't be, Ms. Joan. Have you ever tried talking to Pastor Dickerson about it? Maybe there needs to be some strategies for people connecting more and some real talks about dealing with the heart."

"I haven't. He's got enough to do. I don't want to bother him. I have found an outlet at the center. I wish more of the women would connect too, so they can take off these masks and stop pretending. Then, they won't focus so much on others. I see the center growing to different locations."

"I don't know about that," Hannah said, shaking her head, believing she had done what she was meant to do.

"Oh, it will. I've been praying for you a lot lately, and God showed it to me. He has anointed you for this, dear."

"I used to think so, Ms. Joan, but not anymore," Hannah said, tears flowing. She swiped them away as quickly as they came, not wanting Ms. Joan to see her this way. Ms. Joan assured her it was okay to cry. It was a release. Hannah continued, "I've been through so much in such a short time. Things just keep happening. God allowed me to forgive and reconnect with my aunt, then she passed away not long after that. How can I help women to have faith and trust that God can do anything but fail when I'm so confused right now?"

"Dear, maybe your aunt had fulfilled what she needed to. We won't always understand the things that happen in our lives, but we can still trust in the Lord."

"I just don't get it, Ms. Joan. How much more is going to happen? My husband and I miscarried twice before having Ariel. And I was abused as a child by Aunt Loretta's husband during the time Mama wasn't in my life and Daddy had been kept from seeing me by Mama, so I walked around feeling unwanted for years. Even while married to Levi, I still felt I needed love so much that I tried to adopt my niece when I found out Brittany was pregnant. I wasn't concerned if my sister wanted to keep her. I just wanted a baby because the doctor told me I wouldn't have one."

"Yet, God performed a miracle by giving you and your husband Ariel and in the restoration of your relationship with your mother. Isn't that what you told me?"

"But..."

"But He also gave you the opportunity to spend some time with your aunt and turned your life around so you could help other women," Ms. Joan said, interrupting Hannah. "In times like this, we must remember the character of God. We must remember the love of God. He never said things would be perfect in this fallen world, but He did say he would be with us."

"I guess."

"Hannah, it's okay for us to be angry and disappointed, but even when we're there, we must hand it over to Christ. He can handle it. Haven't you read about David?"

"Yeah. David didn't hold anything back." Hannah laughed.

"That's because God knows what's in our hearts already. We might as well share it."

"I never thought about it like that."

"That's why it's called a relationship," Ms. Joan added.

"True." Hannah nodded in agreement.

"When you are angry with Levi, more than likely, he already knows it because you all have been married for a while, and God has mended your hearts together, even in times of trouble, right?" Ms. Joan asked.

Hannah pondered on that statement for a few seconds. She was a little angry with God about the loss of her aunt. She thought this season of her life would be filled with joy and redemption, but then this curve ball was thrown.

"Thank you so much for your words, Ms. Joan. You remind me so much of Ms. Priscilla. You both speak with such wisdom, and you tell me what I need to hear."

"That's the Lord using us."

"I needed this talk. I was falling into a funk like I had in the past."

"We all do, and the Lord knows, so He uses others."

"He is such a personal God."

"Yes, He is. And watch. He will help you overcome this new hurdle in your life. You know His voice is real."

"Yes, I do. I've kinda been pushing it away since Aunt Loretta passed."

"Don't," Ms. Joan urged. "We need His voice in this unpredictable world. We need Him for direction and guidance."

"That's for sure," Hannah said, nodding again.

A few minutes later, they stood to continue their tour. They laughed and joked. Hannah enjoyed every moment of her time with Ms. Joan. She checked her phone after feeling it vibrate in her crossbody purse. It was her mom.

Give me a call when you get a chance. Hannah wondered what it was.

Keep trusting Me, she heard in her spirit. This time, she remembered what Ms. Joan had just said, "We need God's voice."

Hannah knew she couldn't fix anything on her own. That's why it was easier for her to fold.

Okay, Lord. I hear You. I want to try, but it still doesn't make sense, she said in her heart as they finished out the tour.

CHAPTER TWENTY-FIVE

Friday, June 22

"Thank you, ladies, for meeting with me this afternoon," said Mr. Lewis, Hannah's aunt's lawyer.

She still had no clue as to why her mom asked her to meet her here today. Her mom had even taken off, so she knew it had to be important. She was sure it had to do with what her aunt had left. Her sister, Brittany, had also been invited, but she had to work.

"No problem," Hannah's mom said.

"I don't want to take up too much of your time, so let's jump right in. Ms. Hamilton, I met you recently when you came with your sister when she wanted to give you power of attorney in case something should happen to her."

"Yes, I remember," Hannah's mom said.

Hannah looked at her mom in shock. "Mama, you didn't tell me that."

"I know. She wanted it to be between me and her.

"Well, that day when she met with me, she also made sure the changes she'd made to her trust years ago would be carried out."

"Yes, she said she had made some changes," Hannah's mom said.

"She had a good amount of investments and had been paying more into her accounts before she retired," the lawyer continued.

"Yeah. She told me," Hannah's mom said.

"So, I'll read what she asked me to present to you and your kids."

"Okay," her mom said.

Hannah looked over at her. They both shrugged, not having a clue of what this guy was about to share.

To my dear sister, I know I don't have millions, but if anything ever happens to me, I want you, my nieces, and my nephew to have all of what I have left behind. I can't stop Malcolm from taking the house and the car, but my retirement and investments, I have made some changes to, and I want to leave to you all since we don't have any children.

"Oh, my goodness. I had no clue she'd done this. I mean, she told me she was concerned about her husband getting a hold of her money. My sister didn't have to do this. I wish I could talk to her. She was my only sibling," Hannah's mom cried.

Mr. Lewis stood to hand her a tissue. Hannah moved her chair closer to hold her mom's hand.

"Yes. She was adamant about changing her beneficiaries, so she left a portion of her retirement to you, which equals to about fifty thousand dollars." Hannah's mom gasped, and Hannah's eyes widened.

"Are you sure?" her mom asked.

"Yes. I've run the numbers more than once already, and the rest of her retirement is to be split between your kids. This totals $25,000."

"Oh, my God. That is a blessing, but I would rather have my aunt," Hannah cried.

"What about her husband?" her mom asked. "Can't he go after that money?"

"Not if it was already spelled out in her trust and she made the changes to who would be her beneficiaries. The state of Georgia is not what's called a community property state, so he is not entitled to 50% of her earnings, savings, or life insurance like some states."

"Wow," Hannah said, not knowing what else to say. She wished they didn't have to have this conversation.

"Hold on," Mr. Lewis said. "That's not all."

"What?" Hannah's mom asked with a baffled look.

"The remaining amount has been left to the So That You May Live Women's Development Center."

"What?" Hannah said, standing, her mouth opened in surprise. "My part of the $25,000 is plenty to help out for now. There's more?"

"Yes, ma'am. Your aunt called me not long ago. She planned to take this money out to give to you, but she didn't know if you would accept it, so she wanted to wait a little while. When she started getting those harassing messages..."

"Wait. What?" Hannah asked, more surprised now.

"Yes, she asked me to add the final amount to be left to the center. I asked her if everything was okay, and she said she just didn't want her husband to get his hands on her money. She said he would misuse it."

"Why would she leave money to the center?"

"She said that's what was on her heart. She left the remaining balance from her life insurance policy after her burial expenses. This totals fifty thousand dollars."

Hannah's heart raced, "I can't believe this."

"Believe it," Mr. Lewis said.

"Auntie, I wish I could talk to you," Hannah cried, leaning forward with her head in her hands. "I can't believe this." She could hear her mom crying as well. "By the way, I'm planning to close the center at the end of the year, but I will continue to go around and minister and mentor women all over, just not with the intense responsibility of the day-to-day operations. Someone else can do that. I'll just come in and share with the already established ministries. The money will be used in that capacity."

"No, she left it to finance the building you are running."

"I don't plan to keep it open. This has been too traumatic for me," Hannah said.

"I understand," said Mr. Lewis. She wanted me to read this part to you, Hannah."

Hannah, my beautiful niece, I know I can't make up for my part in hurting you and staying with such a monster all these years. I want to give you something to help with the center. Please continue helping those women and even girls as God leads. It is a work that needs to be done. So, if anything were to ever happen to me, please accept these additional funds. Don't do it for me. Do it for those women and those who will follow. You are amazing. As I told you before, I'm proud of you. It's not a lot, but I hope it can help.

With all my love, Aunt Loretta

***

After climbing into their separate cars, Hannah and her mom left the lawyers office. She was still speechless. She and her mom talked to each other on the phone as they drove. They were still baffled by what her aunt had done without Malcolm knowing. Hannah believed he had an idea of $125,000 she had saved over the years. That was why he wouldn't sign the divorce papers and had taken her life. Hannah was a little uneasy about the amount that had been left to her. She'd received more than the rest of them. Her mom told her not to worry because her aunt had the right to do whatever she wanted to with her money. Plus, it was needed, so her mom had no complaints, and she assured Hannah that her sister and brother wouldn't either.

Hannah then began to think about the things she would be able to purchase for the center when the money was released, but she still didn't want to keep it open. Mr. Lewis had said it could take several months to receive the funds.

She and her mom decided to go to her mom's apartment to plan for the center for the rest of the year before it was time for her to pick up Ariel from daycare. Her mom said she would make some chicken alfredo since it was a quick meal. Hannah loved her mom's homemade alfredo sauce. She also promised to make Hannah a strawberry upside-down cake to take home for her, Levi, and Ariel. She hung up with her mom to call Levi and tell him about her aunt's generosity. He didn't pick up, so she left him a voice text and reminded him of how much she loved and appreciated him.

The provision for the center was made, but Hannah just didn't have the motivation to move forward after December. If she couldn't use the money the way she had explained to her aunt's attorney, she would instruct him to donate it to different charities for women. Her heart was shattered after the loss of her aunt, and she was haunted by the tragedy. She had to close the center and move on with her life.

CHAPTER TWENTY-SIX

Saturday, July 11

Hannah had pulled off the biggest event since opening up the center, the success fair. She and her mom had done most of the planning for the community success fair, but Ms. Joan, April, and Amara had stayed later at the center over the past three weeks to pull together the pieces of the event. Hannah was excited because she wasn't limited to using the center or having it outside in the raging Georgia heat. Her family had come together and helped her book an indoor event hall not far from her house.

Tons of people had shown up, and they were only an hour into it. Even Fox 5 Atlanta was in attendance and had interviewed her about her vision for the event and asked her to provide information on how to donate to the center. She couldn't believe it. More funding would be provided to the center, but she still couldn't get passed everything that had happened to consider remaining opened.

As Hannah waited for her husband to return from taking their daughter to the restroom, she stood back and continued to take it all in. Her aunt's final words came back to her, "Tell them to live. Tell them for me.." The words repeated in her mind.

Lord, how can I? I don't have the strength, nor the motivation, Hannah prayed to herself.

Won't you just trust me with all that concerns you? She heard in her spirit. *I will heal your heart once again. Lead my women out of captivity.*

I don't know if I can.

Give me your hand, and I will lead you.

I will try.

After praying in her heart and hearing from God, she took in the space. She was proud of what had unfolded before her eyes. God had given her more favor than she deserved. This event would help so many.

Her volunteers April, Amara, and Ms. Joan were assisting the participants in different locations around the room. Her mom and mother-in-law were sharing a booth filled with their tasty southern foods they had spent days preparing. There were several other booths set up around the perimeter of the room. A few job agencies who were mostly hiring for warehouse work and several restaurants were there—Zaxby's, Chick-fil-A, and McDonald's were the fast-food restaurants in attendance. Next to them were the health check booths with nurses from Piedmont hospital, a few colleges were next to them, and one trade school Hannah wasn't familiar with. She was unable to get anyone from her OB/GYN's office to attend, but her long-time doctor, Dr. Sarin, sent lots of educational material to pass out, and Hannah had the information for women to sign up for their yearly exams. She had also told Hannah how proud she was of her. Dr. Sarin had been there through much of her journey of ups and downs. Her words meant a lot to Hannah.

Across from the colleges and trade school was the community resource booth. Hannah thought that was a great addition to the success fair. The booth had information for the local food banks, shelters, mental health services, and childcare assistance. That was also where the housing help was located. Over in the corner next to it was a police booth. Hannah had asked if a few off-duty officers would be able to come and answer any questions that the women or any others in attendance might have about their rights or how to get help if they needed it. This was inspired by the loss of her aunt. She also planned to add self-defense classes at the center. In addition to this, the friend who had helped her get her grants was hosting an entrepreneur start-up workshop in the room next to where they were.

"Your child is greedy," Levi said, returning with their daughter.

"What are you talking about?"

"Mommy, can I go get a treat from my nanas' table?"

"Not right now, Ariel. You just ate when you got here," Hannah said.

"But Daddy, my tummy will be happy," said Ariel, turning to her dad for him to take her side.

"Get your child," Levi said, laughing.

"So, she's my child when she's like this, huh?" Hannah asked, pretending to box with her husband.

"And is," Levi said.

"Okay. I'm going to remember that."

"You need a pen to write it down?" her husband said, always the joker.

"Mommy, please."

"Not right now, Ariel. Now come over here and have a seat," Hannah said, pointing to the round table next to where they stood.

Ariel marched over with her arms folded, slamming herself in one of the chairs, then laying her head on her hands as if she'd lost her favorite toy.

"It looks like another big crowd is starting to show up. This event turned out nice, my girl boss,"

Levi said, kissing Hannah on the cheek.

"It did. I'm still floored by the turnout."

"It sure has things people need."

"I know. I've never known of anything hosted like this."

"Look at you being a trailblazer. God is doing big things through you."

"I know, but I'm still not sure I want to continue, Levi."

"You are anointed for this, Peter. Don't disobey God. Let Him heal you as you continue to go, babe. This is part of your water-walking experience," Levi said, referring to one of Jesus' disciples, Peter, who He commanded to walk on water, and he had done so as long as he kept his eyes on Jesus.

"I guess I've only been paying attention to the raging sea around me and almost drowned."

"Almost doesn't matter, babe," said Levi.

"Pray for me to grip Christ's hand. That's the only way I can keep going. I'm just realizing I had loosened it a bit after losing Aunt Loretta."

"Already on it," Levi said.

"Keep an eye on Busy Bee while I walk around a bit, okay."

"You better hope I don't give her away as a donation," Levi said, grinning.

"I'm not worried about you giving my child away. You want to live to see another day," Hannah said, walking across the room.

"That's not Christlike, ma'am," she heard Levi say, making her burst into laughter.

A lady she was passing gave her a strange look. Hannah smiled at her and kept walking. She asked if anyone needed anything as she passed each booth. Each said no. She kept going until she reached the space where her friend's entrepreneur workshop was being held. There were a few men and women in there. Hannah listened in as she shared some nuggets.

"Make sure you know who your audience is ahead of time—no, your audience is not everyone. Also, know what services or products you want to offer. Decide what you're passionate about. God didn't place us here to do everything because that's how we get burned out and don't follow through with anything."

"What if you feel that you have multiple gifts?" a woman at the front asked.

"You may have multiple gifts, but what God has placed in you is connected. For example, I direct a few women's centers in another area, but I also speak to women about the topics we discuss at the centers. I also host things like this, showing people how to start a business. They are all connected. They are not things that are vastly different. For example, I don't direct the women's centers, sell body products, and sell life insurance. There is nothing wrong with any of that, but sometimes people get into those things just because the money sounds good, but that may not be their calling."

"I got you," the woman in the audience said.

Hannah listened for a few more minutes, then she headed back around to where the booths were located. She stopped to talk to the trade school and the colleges about how the women at her center could get grants. One of the college recruits gave her their information and offered to come over and host a workshop on grant funding and other ways to go to school without mounds of debt.

As she was stepping away, Hannah was being called to the stage. One of the representatives from Chick-fil-A and one of the nurses from Piedmont stood with a piece of foam board in each of their hands. Maybe they wanted to thank her for hosting this event. After reaching the stage they asked the individuals in the room to give Hannah a round of applause.

Ah, what are they about to do?

The representative of Piedmont spoke first. "Mrs. Jefferson, after we were asked to come here today and serve the community with you, we decided we wanted to give a donation to your center as a token of our appreciation. We would like to donate five hundred dollars toward the work you are doing for the women in this community."

"You didn't have to do that. Thank you so much," Hannah said, hugging the nurse.

"And we would like to add this twelve-hundred-dollar check," the representative of Chick-fil-A said.

"I appreciate you all. I didn't expect this," Hannah said, hugging the other representative. She was thankful she could return most of her family's money to them right away for funding this event. *Okay, Lord. You are speaking loud and clear. I'm gripping your hand,* Hannah prayed in her heart. *Help me not to crumble. Help me to obey and not rebel.*

After another hour of assisting the people who came in and taking several pictures with the other participants at the event, it was time for Hannah's closing remarks. She stood in the middle of the room and thanked each of the participants and the attendees who remained. She encouraged the attendees to follow up with whatever organization they'd signed up with.

"This event exceeded my expectations for sure. I would love to consider doing this every year for the community of Forest Park," Hannah said. "Today was proof that there is much work to be done, and I thank God for choosing me to play a role through the So That You May Live Women's Development Center. Please reach out if you are in need of our services. Most of all, I encourage you to grow in your purpose and *live* the life God has placed you here to live. Keep going, no matter what. Don't give up on yourself, and never let anyone hinder you from accepting your value because you were made in God's image and likeness.

Walk in it."

"Babe, that was beautiful," her husband said, embracing her.

"Thank you, husband."

"Good job, Mommy," Ariel said, looking up at Hannah.

"Thank you, Busy Bee," Hannah replied, kneeling to kiss her daughter on the cheek.

"Now can I get a treat?" Ariel asked.

"You just don't give up do you, little girl?" Levi said.

"She does not," Hannah said.

As Hannah got Ariel a treat from her mother and mother-in-law's table, Levi and a few of the other men helped the participants take down their tables. Hannah was grateful for the success, more donations, and connections, but she was ready to get home and rest. Her work here was done, but Monday would soon arrive.

CHAPTER TWENTY-SEVEN

Friday, July 17

After her news interview had aired, the center received in another $32,000 in donations.

Hannah's mind was blown. It would take several more months for them to receive the money from her aunt's trust, but God already knew that, so He moved on the hearts of those in her community and others to give. She couldn't understand why she had such trouble acquiring more grants and experienced theft of the centers donations prior to this time, but she further understood this was a lesson in trusting. *Okay, Lord. I will obey.* You are amazing in all your ways. Hannah was eternally grateful for what she had been able to do with the incoming funds. The first thing she did was set aside an emergency fund for what-ifs. She planned to add more once the other trust money was released.

Hannah had been working since early morning. After an hour of research, she had placed an order for five refurbished computers from Secondhand Systems, Inc. They had great reviews and even had some video demonstrations from those who had purchased from them. Hannah was excited.

Anything else would be better than the clunky old ones she had now. She had also purchased a yearly subscription for Coursera. It contained a wide range of career-related topics, and the women could take some short online courses and gain certificates. At least, this was a start—a great new beginning.

The only other thing she had paid for was today's financial empowerment workshop. They were coming to the end of a fifteen-minute break. The center was bursting at the seams today. Many women had shown up, and most of them seemed to be in a cheerful mood. Hannah was thankful she was only assisting with replenishing their snacks, so she could enjoy the workshop herself for a change.

Mr. Brian Cambridge, a guy who was connected with Dr. Taylor, the woman who had helped her acquire the first set of grants she'd received, was here to presenting. He was a banker. From what he'd shared with her when they talked earlier in the week, he was quite knowledgeable of the topic of finance. He had already dropped several nuggets in the first hour and a half.

Hannah's husband, Levi, had taken off so he could attend. He had told her, "You can never learn too much about finances." Mama Jefferson was gracious enough to take care of Ariel for them for the millionth time. Hannah couldn't thank her mother-in-law enough. Ms. Joan, Amara, Simone, April, and several other women were in attendance. Her mother couldn't make it because she wasn't feeling well. Hannah was worried about her. She planned to check on her afterward.

"Alright, is everyone ready to get started again?" Mr. Cambridge asked.

"Yes," several of the women yelled.

"Alright, so far, we have covered the basics: giving, budgeting, saving, and investing. Because we are what..." Mr. Cambridge said, pointing the mic at the audience.

"We are Kingdom citizens."

So That You May Live

"That's right. Being a part of God's Kingdom, we are helping to finance the Kingdom to assist in spreading the gospel. Well, in this next hour, we are going to dig into budgeting. I'm sure many of you know something about budgeting, but we can always learn more."

"See, great minds think alike," Levi said, looking at Hannah.

"Really?" Hannah asked, laughing.

"Pay attention to the man. He's getting ready to share," Levi said, nudging Hannah.

"I hope you're taking notes because I've got some more good stuff for you," said Mr. Cambridge.

"Got my notebook," Amara said, lifting hers in the air.

"Good. Now, the first thing you should do is begin tracking your expenses. Start writing down your expenses for one month, then you will be able to target where your money is going. I'm sure there is an app out there that you could use, but I love to use good ole pencil and paper."

"Yes, the old school has always been the best way," Ms. Joan said, smiling.

"Amen to that," Mr. Cambridge said. "Next, I want you to set clear goals for why you are choosing to remain on a strict budget. It could be to pay off a debt, saving for a vacation, or simply to have a savings and not just spending everything on bills. When you come up with your budget, I want you to make sure you identify the needs versus the wants. That's important."

"That's true," one of the women said out loud as she took notes.

"You don't want to have all these wants and push aside your needs. That's a way of keeping you in debt."

"Can you give us an example?" Amara asked.

"Well, if there is a credit card bill, for example, that needs to be paid off, but you keep putting it off for those things on that want list…Those things could wait. We want to get rid of as much debt as possible. It lightens our loads. Wouldn't you all agree?"

"Amen," Hannah said, thankful she was still riding in her paid-off car. What if she or Levi would have purchased a new one? Her experience opening and running the center over these last few months would have been worse.

"Alright. Another tip I want to give you is to divide your household expenses into categories. For example, you could have mortgage or rent, groceries, car, utilities, and entertainment. Even if you are working toward getting a house or apartment, you have to have a budgeting plan so you don't struggle."

"Got it," Amara said.

Hannah knew she was working hard to find her a place to live and to move out of the shelter soon. Hannah and Pastor Gibson were working with her to find resources that could assist her.

"Now, you want to allocate at least twenty percent of your income to saving something for yourself."

"I want to get to that place one day. When I get on my feet, I may only be able to save maybe five percent of what I make. That's being realistic," said Crystal, a woman from Hannah's church who had only been at the center once or twice.

"Listen, I understand. We all have to start somewhere, so if five percent is what works best for you starting off, then save that. I just want you ladies to put aside something in case something comes up in your life. There are several trending *Easy Ways to Save* videos on social media. Check them out. I'm sure some of them will come in handy for you."

"Thanks so much for that," Crystal said, writing down what Mr. Cambridge had shared.

"There's one other thing I want to talk about before I stop and allow you to work on this list I have given you. I want you to challenge yourself to open a savings account if you don't have one. Then, I want you to set up an automatic transfer of a small portion of your payroll check into that account. Even if it is twenty dollars to start off, I want you to take the challenge."

"That sounds great," Simone said. "I'm in my mid-twenties, so I'm still learning about this stuff.

Would I go to my manager at my job to have this set up?"

"The manager should be able to direct you to the right person to help you."

"Thanks!"

"Now ladies, we are going to take some time right here to write out those goals, create a way you are going to track those expenses, and put them into categories. You will also be able to decide what or if you can start saving something."

"Yes. I'm ready," Simone said, doing a little cheer in her seat.

As the ladies worked, Hannah walked around to see if she could get them anything or if Mr. Cambridge needed anything else. As she neared the front window, she thought she saw someone outside.

Who can that be?

"Babe, who is that?" Levi asked, walking up behind her.

Once Hannah reached the front window, her heart raced, finding Tamela sitting on the curb right outside the door.

"I know she did not show up here," Hannah whispered, walking to the door, her husband following.

A few of the women looked up when she turned around to let April and Mr. Cambridge know that she'd be right back. Levi stepped outside with her. Tamela sat with her back to them and her head hung low.

Trying to remain civil, Hannah said a prayer to herself before speaking. "Tamela, what are you doing here? How could you show your face here after what you've done, and you lied on my now deceased aunt?" The woman didn't respond at first. Hannah walked closer. She was crying. "Tamela, why are you here?"

"I came to apologize to you," Tamela said through sniffles.

"Apologize? You are going to have to do more tha—"

"Levi, let me handle this," Hannah said, cutting her husband off. "You are going to have to do more than apologize. You are lucky that officer said he couldn't pursue a case against you. You made it look like I gave you that money. Why would you pretend to be my friend and a woman of God?"

"I'm so sorry, Hannah," Tamela cried, her head still bowed.

"Sorry is not enough, Tamela. Not only did you take a portion of my donations for my center, you made me suspicious of my aunt because you knew about my past experiences, and you lied and said I was paying you back a loan I owed you. You know that's not true, and why in the world would you get your family member involved, risking her freedom?"

"I was wrong. I was desperate."

"So, you steal from your 'best' friend and from these other women who come here for help and make up a lie about my aunt?" Hannah screamed. Levi moved toward her.

"I'm so sorry, Hannah," Tamela said, now standing and facing Hannah.

"You said that already, and you can keep it and leave. I can't do this with you."

"Is everything okay?" Ms. Joan asked, stepping out to check on them.

"Hannah, please listen. I promise to pay it back. I've asked God to forgive me for what I've done."

"We're okay, Ms. Joan," Hannah said, turning to look at her.

"Okay. Let me know if you need anything."

"Okay. Levi, can you see if they need any help inside while I finish here?"

"Babe, if you think I'm going to leave you out here with someone who stole thousands of dollars from you and pretended to be your friend, I wish I would."

"Honey, please can you go inside?"

"Hannah, I'm not moving. I'll peep my head inside from out here."

"Benard left me several months ago, and I was left trying to figure out how I would pay for my apartment," Tamela explained. "He said he was tired of carrying the load while I continued to spend and purchase things we couldn't afford."

"Wait. I'm confused. You made it seem like he was okay paying for everything," Hannah said.

"I lied. I wanted you to think that because I was envious of you."

"Of me? Why?"

"You were able to step out of the classroom and start your own business, and your husband supported you one hundred percent. You seemed to have the perfect life and everything you wanted, and I only had the things I'd purchased. They made me feel valuable. I've never felt a real sence of purpose within me, except for being a wife, then Bernard left me."

"I can't believe what I'm hearing," Levi said.

Hannah held up her hand for him to let her handle it.

"So let me get this straight: Instead of you getting a full-time job in order to pay your bills when he left you, you stole thousands of dollars from me?"

"It seemed easier at the time. I needed money fast."

"Really?"

"Yes," Tamela said, looking away. "I still ended up losing the apartment. Now, I'm living out of a hotel room."

"Why the cousin's account?" Hannah asked, not feeling any remorse for Tamela.

"She didn't know Benard had left me. I don't tell my family my business."

"But you use them," Hannah said, disgusted by Tamela's actions.

"I was wrong, and I've asked God to forgive me for it all. I made her think he was always working when I would talk to her. And...well, I didn't think I would ever get caught because I was able to erase the evidence of those funds ever being there. I would leave some of the money and took the rest."

"But it didn't delete. PayPal retrieved the records. You didn't know that."

"I didn't know that was possible."

"Obviously," Hannah said, growing more annoyed by the minute. "And how did you get my login info?" She had to know the truth.

"One day when you had logged into your account but had to go to the restroom really bad. I watched you come out and pretended I was going in there to put away something. Your Paypal account was opened on your computer, so I went in and turned off the notifications and sent the larger donations to my cousin's account as payments. I had already set up everything. I was just waiting on the opportunity to gain access. I knew I would eventually because you were always distracted with something to do for the center. I had many opportunities during the workshops you hosted."

"Tamela, I trusted you. How could you do something like that to me, to anybody?"

"I was desperate," Tamela said, tears flowing again. "I needed money right away."

"So, how do you plan to pay the money back to the center?" Hannah asked, turning around to see if Levi was still there. He was. She should have known that her husband was serious about not moving.

"I still have some of it. I can transfer it back."

"Oh, no. That account was closed, and I'm not given you access to anything connected to my personal info or my center's."

"I understand."

"I hope you do," Hannah said. "I'll find out a safe way for you to return the funds you have to me."

"Okay. You will probably never forgive me."

"I'm commanded by God to forgive you, Tamela. Will I allow you to ever assist here or anywhere again? That's a hard no."

Trust me, Hannah heard in her spirit. She knew God was referring to Tamela.

Lord, not now.

"I understand," Tamela said, turning and walking toward her car in the parking lot across from the center.

Pray for her, Hannah heard.

Huh? Really, Lord?

Pray for her, God spoke again.

Seriously? But she stole from me.

Forgive as I have forgiven you.

Hannah's shoulders slumped in surrender. This walk was not easy, but she knew if she was to serve women, she had to allow God to lead. Even though she didn't understand what He was doing in this moment, she called out to Tamela and walked toward her. Grabbing the hands of her former friend, Hannah prayed for the woman she once trusted. Tamela cried and fell into Hannah's arms. She led her back over to the door of the center and continued praying. She asked God to help Tamela to trust in Him and not lean to her own understanding. Hannah asked God to heal Tamela every place she hurt and make a way for her. Finally, Hannah asked God to help her to not hold the sin that He'd forgiven Tamela for in her heart.

At that moment, He reminded her of how He had delivered her from herself and her own ways several years ago.

Redemption is for all who will receive it.

Lord, help me to do Your will and not my own, was all Hannah could say in her heart, overwhelmed by His love for Tamela. She knew that every day was a process, but He'd never failed as long as she'd responded.

Yes, God was up to something. He wanted to heal, deliver, and set free the women of Forest Park and every corner of His earth, to help them to find their purpose in Him.

He who is without sin, let him cast the first stone, she finally heard before surrendering and leading Tamela into the center where the other women joined Hannah in embracing her and loving on her as Christ would. Her husband wasn't happy because of all of what Tamela had done to her, but Hannah explained that God had led her to it, so He would guide her through it with His wisdom.

CHAPTER TWENTY-EIGHT

Friday, September 7

A few months had passed since her aunt's death and God's provision for the So That You May Live Women's Development Center, and He continued to provide more funds through those who had now partnered and were giving monthly donations. More news coverage had played an intricate role in this happening. Hannah was now even receiving a small salary, but her husband reminded her that more was coming. She thought about his words when she first decided to step out and obey the Lord—"You will have a salary from the center. Don't you worry."

Hannah smiled as she reflected. She was thankful she didn't walk away. Levi and the rest of her circle had believed for her when she couldn't see it and when she felt she couldn't continue.

God is so faithful, she thought as she drove to a much-needed getaway, singing the older gospel tune "Every Praise" by Hezekiah Walker as it bumped loud through her car speakers.

To celebrate her continued success, Hannah had planned a So That You May Live Women's Weekend of Refreshing in Destin, Florida. Amara, Ms. Joan, April, and her mother-in-law had helped her to plan everything out. They had received enough funds for the center to pay for the Airbnb, so the women only had to cover the gas.

Hannah, her mom, Ms. Priscilla, and her aunt Melissa, her dad's brother's wife, had agreed to work together and cook over this weekend, so the women didn't have to stress about purchasing food. Her mother-in-law couldn't be here. She had an event with her church that weekend, and her sister couldn't come due to work again. Hannah prayed her sister's hours would reduce one day so she could hang out with her more.

The extra donations were also enough to purchase the large-ticket food items. God's timing was perfect, and He continued to provide the manna.

No, You have provided so much more than manna, Hannah thought as she turned off the highway to get some more gas. She wished it could have lasted because she only had about an hour and a half left to drive. She had gotten on the road a little later because she had to wait for Levi to arrive. He had planned a daddy/daughter weekend with Ariel. Her daughter had cried as if Hannah was leaving forever. She assured her little busy bee that she'd be back in a few days.

I wish I could have brought her with me.

As she came out of the gas station from paying, her phone rang.

"Hey, Mama."

"How far away are you?"

"About an hour and a half. What about you all?" Hannah asked.

"We are about thirty minutes away. I am so excited. I needed this time," her mom said.

"Yes, Lord," Ms. Priscilla said in the background.

"Mama, who else is with you?"

"Amara and Simone," she said, referring to two of the women who attended and had now become volunteers at the center.

"Okay, good. April said she would bring two other ladies she knew who she thought would benefit from this weekend. And Ms. Joan is driving up on her own. I have to pick up Aunt Melissa from the airport by nine this evening."

"Okay, and when is Minister Belinda arriving?" her mom asked.

"She'll be here tomorrow. Pastor Richardson said she is a powerhouse. She has taught at several women's conferences."

"I can't wait to hear her. I need a fresh Word," her mom added.

***

By the next morning, everyone had arrived except Minister Belinda. She would be there by noon. It was seven a.m., and Hannah was done with her Bible reading and journaling. She journaled Matthew 7:24–27 about a person building their house on the rock, and the rain, floods, and winds came but it didn't fall. This was connected to hearing and obeying God. As Hannah walked around the breathtaking five-bedroom, six-bathroom remodeled home a few blocks from the beach, she thought about the scripture she'd studied as she remembered that Florida was known for hurricanes.

As beautiful as this place is, can it withstand hurricane force winds and rain? Nothing can save it from the force of nature. This helps me understand how much more I need to remain in Christ, the rock of salvation. I don't have to understand everything, and when things happen, because they will, I give it to Him and allow Him to give me direction. In life, trouble will form just like a hurricane, but I can only stand and keep moving if we are in Christ. Lord, help me to help the women to see this over this weekend as you have shown me.

"Good morning, sweetness," Ms. Priscilla said, entering the oversized living room, bringing Hannah out of her thoughts.

"Good morning, Ms. Priscilla. Did you get some good rest?"

"Oh, yes. I've never been to Destin before. This house and Destin overall are beautiful," Ms.

Priscilla said, waving her hands and turning in a circle, taking it all in. "I will have to come back for sure."

"I would love if we could make this a yearly event," Hannah said.

"Sounds good to me. The Lord will provide as you have already witnessed, and I'm so glad you chose to see it through. I know you've experienced a lot over the years, but God will use it for good and for His glory as you continue to minister to women from all walks of life."

"Yes, He will," Hannah's mom said, joining them.

"Good morning, Ms. Tamika," Ms. Priscilla said, hugging her tight.

"Good morning, Ms. Priscilla. I have enjoyed my time with you already. That late-night talk was so good."

"You're welcome, sweetheart. Anytime."

"I might hold you to that now."

"Please do," Ms. Priscilla said, laughing.

Hannah went to see if Aunt Melissa was awake so they could get a quick breakfast prepared for everyone. Aunt Melissa joined them a few minutes later. As Ms. Priscilla and Aunt Melissa prepared bacon, eggs, and hash browns, Hannah and her mom set out the folding chairs around the room to prepare for their first activities. They all ate quickly so they could get dressed and get started.

After all ten of them had eaten and chatted, Hannah stood and gave a brief overview of what the weekend of women's refreshing was all about. Next, they held hands and prayed, each woman praying whatever came to her heart. Then, Ms. Joan led them in worship, singing the "Goodness of God" by CeCe Winans. Warm tears ran down Hannah's cheeks as she thought about God's goodness toward her and the other women. She also thought about how much He loved her Aunt Loretta as well, and now she was with Him. Oh, how she missed her.

Following a few more worship songs, Hannah hosted the first workshop on living using the acronym that God had given her for the center. She took the time to explain what each letter of the L.I.V.E. acronym represented since they had two new women present: "The *L* stands for learning about Christ. The *I* stands for improving our view of ourselves. The *V* is for finding our voice, and the *E* is for empowering other women and girls to do the same."

Hannah walked over to the island counter and grabbed her small planting pot with soil inside of it. She showed it to the women and the pack of seeds she had in her pocket. Hannah demonstrated planting the seed in the pot. She explained, "Just like a seed needs nourishment to grow, we need Christ to nourish our souls and to grow and walk in what He created us to do."

"Amen," Aunt Melissa said.

"Now, I want you to take a minute and list those things you have lived for and loved more," Hannah instructed, asking her mom and Amara to pass out the paper, clipboards, and pens.

"Oooh, that's deep," said Erica, one of April's guests.

"Yes, it is. We must do this because it's easy for us to live for others and love others more than Christ. When I struggled getting pregnant, God used Ms. Priscilla to help me understand that I needed to love and desire Christ more than being a mother. I can be honest: That was hard to do, but I couldn't do it in my own strength."

"And I desired a relationship with my dad and the husband I lost more than Christ," Hannah's mom said. "That's why I drank so much."

"Really, Ms. Tamika?" Simone asked.

"Yes, ma'am."

Instead of redirecting the women back to the paper they should be writing on, Hannah allowed them to continue talking.

Lord, this is good. We need to learn to be completely honest in order to be set free. If only Aunt Loretta would have been brave enough to do so. Help me to honor her memory through the events you birth through me, Hannah prayed with sadness in her heart as she looked around the room, absent of her aunt's presence.

After their discussion, Hannah, her mom, and Ms. Priscilla prayed with the women one on one about their desire to draw closer and live for Christ. They then talked about the real hindrances that could keep them from giving their hearts to Him.

Next, Hannah grabbed the small puzzle she had put together the night before. She held it up. "Okay, ladies, who can tell me how this puzzle relates to improving ourselves?"

"*Ummm,* each piece could represent a skill within us that could be improved or even a talent we don't even realize we have," Simone said.

"You are on point. And those things all fit together to create a complete picture of what the Lord created us to walk in."

"Come on, now," Ms. Joan said. "You are teaching us good."

"It's all the Lord, Ms. Joan," Hannah said.

"I'm so proud of you," her mom said.

Hannah smiled and blew her mom a kiss. She had the women to draw puzzle pieces on the other piece of paper they'd been provided. She instructed them to add any ideas God was giving them that fit an even greater vision. She told them it could be to complete a trade or take a workshop or class. The women seemed to struggle a little, so she helped them think of what they felt they were being led to do and how they would accomplish it.

Finally, Aunt Melissa assisted Hannah in passing out small mirrors to each woman. She then asked the women to take a few minutes to add positive statements about themselves on a mirror. Hannah participated as she waited for the women to finish. She held hers up and read off a few. "A great teacher and made in God's image."

"I like that one," Amara said. "I'm adding that one."

"Feel free. God's image is actually the most important," Hannah said. "When we accept this, live in Relationship, and understand the love of Christ, no one will be able to diminish our value."

"I'm loving this," Ms. Priscilla said.

As the other women shared what they wrote, Hannah noticed how little they had on their mirrors.

She discussed how important it was to see their own value. Next, she gave each woman a mason jar to decorate with their names. After the women lined their jars across the island, Hannah gave her final instructions for empowering others. "Alright, as we wrap up to get ready to head down to the beach, I would like each woman to add something to another woman's jar by writing something about their value on a slip of paper and placing it into their jar. As we go through the weekend, I want you to add value slips into the jars as God leads you. Don't forget to sign your name, so they'll know who wrote it."

"God has really given you a great vision. You have to do this again," Ms. Joan said.

"I plan to," Hannah said, cleaning up the craft materials.

They rested a while and got dressed so they could leave when Minister Belinda arrived. She had texted Hannah and asked if they could wait for her. Once they all were dressed, they grabbed their towels and walked the few blocks to the beach. Hannah and her small group chatted and laughed more than she ever had before. She learned that Minister Belinda was actually born in Florida, so she loved going to the beach every chance she got. It was a blessing to be among such beautiful spirits. Once they arrived, several of them, including Hannah, weren't brave enough to go too far out into the water because they didn't want to get their hair wet. They wore caps, but Hannah knew beach water and natural hair didn't mix, so she only got wet from her neck down. She and the ladies hung out there for two hours. None of them wanted to leave, but they had to prepare for Minister Belinda's workshop. Hannah knew God would continue speaking through whatever message Minister Belinda would present.

Arriving back at the Airbnb, they all took their showers, had a late lunch, and headed out back.

Hannah and the women all wore sundresses in a variety of colors and styles, and they rocked their wide-brimmed hats to block out the sun. The property was surrounded by palm trees, and they gathered around in chairs to hear Minister Belinda's message, "The Value of Knowing Who You Are in Christ." They all eyed Hannah, a few stating that God was really speaking through them.

"All God," Hannah said, as they set back and took in what else the Lord had to say.

When the message was over, they sat around and talked, getting to know one another more. Finally, they sat on a grass mound, wrapping their arms around one another. Hannah shared Aunt Loretta's last moments and her message to them, "Tell them to live. They have to." Several who knew and spent time with her aunt began to cry, sharing how much they missed her.

Hannah then said, "Ladies, life won't always be that perfectly baked pound cake. It will sometimes include ingredients we never expected to be added, which ruins the entire recipe. It's not for us to judge the women around us. We are called to help our sisters remove those awful ingredients that were added to our recipe, those things that caused us to not be able to identify or accept our true image. We are called to help each other live out God's purpose, see and love who God created, and never allow anyone else to add or subtract from God's recipe of Genesis 1:27. As tears continued to flow, Hannah gave them a few moments to sit in silence. She prayed for each of their strength. When the somber mood lifted, she had them to repeat after her: "I am God's image. I was created for His purpose. I shall live and not die and neither will my purpose die before it's fulfilled." After the women repeated those words, they began to praise God and lift their hands to the sky.

Hannah got their attention after a few moments and continued, "These are our final words of affirmation to ourselves. Repeat after me again, "I vow to live, learn about Christ, to improve my view of myself, find my voice, and empower my other sisters to do the same."

Finally, they hugged one another and found a partner. The partners prayed for each other and vowed to stand together and to hold one another accountable.

Once they were done, they headed back inside. Ms. Priscilla and Hannah's mom made dinner. Then, they decided to take a stroll and walk off the calories. The beautiful Florida weather helped them to all agree that they couldn't spend the remainder of their evening indoors.

Lord, You are awesome in all Your ways, Hannah said in her heart as they all made new friends and memories that would last for years to come.

CHAPTER TWENTY-NINE

Sunday, September 16

The following weekend after returning from their much-needed women's refreshing, Hannah and Levi agreed to her mom hosting a Sunday dinner at their home in memory of Aunt Loretta.

She thought it was needed because it had been a while since they had all gathered together and cut up.

Not having many on her mom's side to invite to the dinner, her mom invited those whom she loved her and had become her family. Her mom read a poem she had written for Loretta and shared memories of them growing up together and even the times they had falling outs. They had cried with her mom and encouraged her to keep moving forward.

Now, as they were sitting to eat, Ariel ran around from person to person, more excited than Hannah had ever seen her. They couldn't all fit around Hannah and Levi's dining table, so they had rented a few long tables they had set up in their living room to enjoy one another. Her mom didn't know about the surprise she and Brittany had cooked up. They were just waiting for the call.

Hannah's mom and mother-in-law had prepared all the food for the soul: collards, smothered chicken, dressing, mac and cheese, yams, and a few cakes.

"Ariel, come over here and eat the rest of your food," Levi said as they tried to finish eating.

"Daddy, I'm talking to Pop Pop," Ariel said, pulling on her dad's arm, thinking she was whispering, trying to get him to give her a piece of cake from the kitchen counter.

"Pass it to me," Hannah's dad said. "I'll try to get her to finish."

"Mommy, I want some more yams," Neveah said to Brittany.

"Okay. Give me a second," Hannah's sister said as she seemed to inhale their mom's dressing.

"Girl, Mama and Mama Jefferson gon' have all us walking around the neighborhood this evening," Hannah said.

"Okay," Brittany added. "She knows it don't make no sense how good this food is."

"Girl, you are so crazy," Hannah said.

"So, what else do you have planned for the center?" Brittany asked.

"I don't know. I will keep you informed of what's coming up. It is keeping me busy."

"Do you ever regret leaving education?" Brittany asked.

"I don't. Yes, these months have been some of the most challenging times of my life, even in comparison of what I endured in the past, but God has been with me every step of the way, and I want to continue to allow him to lead the way. Don't get me wrong, I love the kids I encounter, but this is the season of purpose He has called me into now."

"I agree. You seem more at peace, sis."

"I am."

Brittany's phone rang. "Oh, could this be our call?" Brittany said, lifting her phone. "Hello." She put it on speaker and turned it down a little.

"Hello, sis. How is the dinner going?" Hannah's brother, Malik, asked through FaceTime.

"It is going great. We're having a ball."

"We wish you were here," Hannah added, leaning over.

"You know I can't be there. How is Mama?" he asked.

"She's in the kitchen cleaning, staying busy," Brittany said.

"It has taken a lot of thinking and time away for me to be willing to talk to her," he said.

"Are you ready?" Hannah asked.

"I think so," Malik said.

"Give us a second," Brittany said. She and Hannah headed into the kitchen. "Mama, someone wants to talk to you."

"Who?" her mom asked, turning around and seeing the grins on Hannah's and Brittany's faces.

"See for yourself," Brittany said, handing her mom the phone.

Hannah saw a sparkle in her mom's eye when she saw that it was her brother. Her mom beamed with excitement. "Malik, son."

"I just wanted to check on you. How are you feeling?" Malik asked.

"I'm doing a little better. Loretta's death really hit me hard. How are you, son?"

"I'm doing great. I have a few more years with the Marines, then I can leave if I choose."

"Well, I know you've been very angry with me for what I put you all through as kids, but I am not the same woman I was back then."

"Hannah and Brit told me."

"I'm sorry, son. I truly am," Hannah's mom said, tears flowing. "I miss you. I'm so sorry for everything."

Hannah moved over to wrap her arms around her mom as her brother responded, "You seem like you've changed a lot. I'm sorry for running as far away as I could. I had to get away."

"I don't blame you. I was horrible to you all," her mom said, weeping. "After losing my sister and seeing your granddad still hadn't changed, I knew I couldn't go back to the person I once was. I don't want to be alone without my beautiful kids and grands."

"That's so good to hear," Malik said.

Hannah could tell her brother was uncomfortable talking to their mom, but this was a start.

Hannah looked over and saw her sister crying.

"I would love for us to reconnect when you are ready," her mom continued. "I know it won't be easy, but I'm willing to try."

"I'm looking forward to it. I can't wait to see my two beautiful nieces again too."

"Come get 'em," Brittany said.

Brittany, Malik, Hannah and their mom all burst into laughter.

"I love you, son," Hannah's mom said, wiping away more tears.

Hannah squeezed her mom tighter, trying to comfort her.

"I love you too, Mama."

"We love you too, big head," Hannah said, trying to lighten the mood again.

"Me? Big head?"

"Oh, so you got jokes now? Wait 'til I see you," Hannah added, holding up her fist. "But for real, love you, bro."

"I love you too, sis, and my other big-head sister."

"Love you too," Brittany said, walking over and standing behind their mom so Malik could see her.

After her brother disconnected, Hannah sandwiched between her mom and sister as they held each other for several seconds.

"Lord, I thank You," her mom said as they headed back into the living room.

Her dad, Levi, and Uncle Joseph were cracking jokes about basketball. Aunt Melissa, Ms.

Joan, and Mama Jefferson were sitting out back talking about getting better, not getting older. Hannah laughed as they teased her about how she had a way to go before *old* would even be a part of her vocabulary.

Once the long tables were cleared of food and Ariel and Neveah had gone out back to swing, Levi challenged them to a game of UNO.

"Don't go for it," Hannah said. "He likes to cheat."

"Now, babe, you're a Christian woman. How you gon' tell that lie like that?"

"Y'all are crazy," Brittany said.

"No. That's your sister trying to lie on me because I beat the brakes off her the last time we played."

"You are a brakes lie," Hannah said, playfully punching her husband in the arm.

"Okay, well let's go then," Levi replied.

"Come on, Brit. Let's shut his mouth," Hannah said.

"Come with it. Pops Monroe, you got my back?" Levi asked her dad.

"Yes, son. Let's g'on put a whooping on them."

"Really, Daddy. So, you gon' turn on your daughter for your son-in-law?"

"Stop hating. Mama Tamika, come and get your daughter," Levi said, laughing.

As they sat to play a few rounds of UNO, Hannah's heart was filled with joy. She was walking out God's purpose, had the freedom to go in whatever direction He would lead, and she was surrounded by all the love anyone could hope for.

EPILOGUE

A year later, Hannah stood in the entrance of her new location. With the money her aunt had left and the continued monthly donations, she was able to rent a larger space that had been a church. She had prayed for it, and God had delivered. Now, she could do more for the women in her community. The space had a large room that had once been the sanctuary, and there were four small rooms for meetings. Hannah was grateful for the favor she'd received on the monthly cost. Because the space had been sitting for almost a year, the seller took money off the lease.

Hannah had set up for the lease payment to automatically come out of the business account, and she assured that it and her PayPal account had several layers of protection. She examined them every chance she got. There was so much she had learned on this entrepreneurial journey, and God continued to teach her more.

Hannah's tribe of supporters were there with her as usual—even Tamela came to wish her well. They hadn't returned to the friendship they once had, and Tamela wasn't allowed to assist at the center anymore, but God had led Hannah to invite her to the activities she hosted there every now and then. Hannah and her mom moved forward as she led the crowd into the foyer of the So That You May Live Women's Development Center's new location. At the entry of the sanctuary area stood a lavender and black balloon arch she'd had made. Lavender and black balloons were also at the entrance and taped to the walls around them. She stood in the center of the foyer as she told her family, friends, and other attendees about the vision and additional programs offered, one being self-defense. She introduced her longtime volunteer and friend, April, as her assistant and new receptionist, and Ms. Joan and Amara as her volunteers.

Once the noise level died down, Hannah explained to the crowd about the loss of her aunt who had helped at the center a short time but had done an amazing job helping to empower the women.

"To honor my Aunt Loretta, I have created a fifteen-hundred-dollar scholarship that will be given away each year to assist a woman in need. I have also named our counseling space Loretta's Counseling Corner," Hannah explained, opening the door closest to where she stood.

On the back wall was a beautiful painting of her aunt. She had it made with a photo her mom had of her from a few years back. Around it was the title of the space. Hannah's mom's eyes widened, and her jaw dropped.

"Oh, Hannah. This is beautiful. Thank you for doing this for Loretta."

"You don't have to thank me, Mama. Aunt Loretta will always live in my heart and will be a part of this center."

"This is so beautiful," her mom repeated, tears flowing.

Giving the attendees a few minutes to view the painting, Hannah moved everyone into the sanctuary area for the next presentation behind the large black cloth on the wall. Once everyone was seated in the soft, comfy purple seats, Hannah went to the podium.

"I have one more thing to share. I decided to make the *L.I.V.E.* part of So That You May Live an acronym. I had something behind me painted to represent it. Are you ready to take a look?"

"Yes," a few from the crowd shouted.

April and Amara removed the large cloth and stepped aside. Her dad, husband, and several others in the crowd whistled and made positive comments about how nice it was. Hannah's heart filled with joy. It was a picture of a large flourishing tree with deep roots. Across it read *So That You May L.I.V.E.* with the words representing each letter in parenthesis underneath it.

"This large tree represents being rooted in Christ," Hannah said, pointing to the painting. "The massive roots here are deeply planted into the ground as we are when we walk in relationship with Him.

He teaches us about himself, and He helps us improve the view of ourselves. He also helps us to find our voice, and then and only then can we empower others."

Hannah went on to explain the women's names painted on the leaves of the tree, Aunt Loretta being one of them. She would forever be a part of the vision. Ms. Joan's name was also added. She was now helping to empower other women at the center, having grown by leaps and bounds in just over a year.

Amara was also listed. She had left the shelter, had gotten an income-based apartment and was helping Hannah as much as she could when she wasn't working and taking classes toward her degree in human resource management.

Yes, God had given Hannah a new life in Christ and a new purpose to fulfill, and he would continue to work through her to help other women to experience the same. Yes, her faith had been tested, His true purpose had been revealed, and redemption had been claimed by those who received it.

Your mission hasn't changed, Hannah heard in her spirit. *Like Moses and Joshua, I will use you to lead women out of captivity, into the promise I have for them.*

Continue to use me for Your glory, were Hannah's words back to God.

ABOUT THE AUTHOR

Denise M. Walker Denise M. Walker is a wife, mother, minister, author, educator, podcaster, speaker, workshop host, and entrepreneur. She is the founder of Hope-in-Christ Ministries and the owner of Armor of Hope Writing & Publishing Services, LLC.

Denise is the host of Hope-in-Christ w/Denise Podcast. She also presents Bible literacy/verse mapping, wholeness in Christ topics for women, and My True Identity workshops for at-promise teen girls and women.

Through her business, Denise is a bestselling/award winning author. She has written and published 12 books to date, co-authored several anthologies, and is a contributing author to The Educator Magazine. Denise is also a copyeditor and proofreader for Christian nonfiction authors and children's books. In addition, she is a nonfiction and children's book writing coach.

Contact Denise:

denise@hope-in-christ.com, contact@denisemwalker.com, www.denise.walker.com, www.hope-in-christ.com

Connect with Denise:

@authordenisemwalker, @hope_in_christ_withDenise, @hopeinchristblog, @authordenisemwalker, @hope-in-christ w/Denise Podcast, www.kingdominfluencersbroadcast.com/shows

Other Books By This Author

Denise M. Walker is a multi-genre author. Please check out some of her other books below.

- **YA Teen Fiction**:

  Hannah's Hope (YA)

  Hannah's Heart (Christian Teen Fiction)

- **Bible Journals/Verse Mapping Books:**

  Representing God: Taking a Healthy Look at the Holy One of Israel (Teen workbook on Christ's Deity)

  Is This English Class or Bible Study Book 1 (Verse Mapping Strategies)

  Is this English Class or Bible Study Book 2 (Verse Mapping Strategies)

  The HOPE Method: A 15-Minute Bible Study Strategy

  The HOPE Method: A 30-Minute Bible Study Strategy

  I B.E.E.L.I.E.V.E. Youth Journal

- **Women's Christian Fiction:**

  Barren Womb

  Sufficient Grace

So That you May Live

- **Business Coaching Journal**

(For Christian Nonfiction Authors):

The S.C.R.I.P.T. (An Armor of Hope Manual for Aspiring Christian Authors)

- **Co-Authored Anthologies:**

Influence 365 Devotional (Derashay Zorn - Compiler)

Do It Right the First Time: Publish and Market You Best Seller (Valerie J. Lewis Coleman - Compiler)

Made in the USA
Columbia, SC
01 October 2024